"Five hundr ☐ W9-AWW-758

The silence gave way to murmurs of shock and Alicia lifted a hand to her lips. She recognized the voice instantly.

"Just to be sure I didn't mishear, was that five hundred thousand pounds?"

"Yes."

"Ladies and gentlemen, what a truly exceptional evening. Those of you lucky enough to secure an item—or person—please leave your details and payment at the administration booth near the door."

Alicia waited by the administration desk with nerves that wouldn't calm down. Five hundred thousand pounds? What on earth had he been thinking?

"Good evening, sir. Are you the lucky winner of Miss Griffith's services?"

She barely heard the question. Her ears were ringing and her mind was in free fall at the realization that not only was Graciano here, but that he'd *bid* on her.

"Yes."

"Wonderful. And what was your name, sir?"

Alicia turned slowly, not needing to hear any more to know it was him. Nothing could prepare her for this moment. Not the memories that haunted her, nothing.

"This is Graciano Cortéz," Alicia said quietly.

The Long-Lost Cortéz Brothers

Two powerful men...and the shocking secret that binds them!

In the aftermath of the tragic accident that killed their family, Graciano Cortéz was ripped apart from the younger brother he'd vowed to protect. Graciano has never stopped looking for him, even while he was building his billion-dollar empire from the ground up.

Then, his decades-long search leads him to the palace doors of Sheikh Tariq al Hassan of Savisia... Will he finally be reunited with his long-lost sibling? And will the road to their reunion bring both Graciano and Tariq more than they bargained for—life-changing desire?

After ten years apart, a shocking reunion will force Graciano to face the woman he never forgot and the secret she keeps that will rock his world...

Read Graciano and Alicia's story in
The Secret She Must Tell the Spaniard

Royal advisor Eloise is tasked with approving her queen's suitor, Sheikh Tariq, which is complicated by the undeniable chemistry erupting between *her* and Tariq!

Read Tariq and Eloise's story in
Desert King's Forbidden Temptation
Coming soon!

Clare Connelly

———

THE SECRET SHE MUST TELL THE SPANIARD

HARLEQUIN®
PRESENTS™

ISBN-13: 978-1-335-58419-9

The Secret She Must Tell the Spaniard

Copyright © 2023 by Clare Connelly

For questions and comments about the quality of this book,
please contact us at CustomerService@Harlequin.com.

Harlequin Enterprises ULC
22 Adelaide St. West, 41st Floor
Toronto, Ontario M5H 4E3, Canada
www.Harlequin.com

Printed in U.S.A.

Clare Connelly was raised in small-town Australia among a family of avid readers. She spent much of her childhood up a tree, Harlequin book in hand. Clare is married to her own real-life hero, and they live in a bungalow near the sea with their two children. She is frequently found staring into space—a surefire sign she is in the world of her characters. She has a penchant for French food and ice-cold champagne, and Harlequin novels continue to be her favorite-ever books. Writing for Harlequin Presents is a long-held dream. Clare can be contacted via clareconnelly.com or on her Facebook page.

Books by Clare Connelly

Harlequin Presents

Crowned for His Desert Twins
Emergency Marriage to the Greek
Pregnant Princess in Manhattan

Passionately Ever After...

Cinderella in the Billionaire's Castle

Signed, Sealed...Seduced

Cinderella's Night in Venice

The Cinderella Sisters

Vows on the Virgin's Terms
Forbidden Nights in Barcelona

Visit the Author Profile page
at Harlequin.com for more titles.

CHAPTER ONE

'I'M SO SORRY, I...' The apology died on Alicia Griffiths' lips as she looked up, and up, past a broad chest, wide shoulders and tanned neck, into a face that was not only familiar to her but burned into her retinas.

Despite the fact ten years had passed, there was no mistaking the man before her.

Graciano Cortéz.

The ground beneath her feet seemed to give way. She lifted a hand to the fine necklace she wore, looping her finger through the chain and pulling it from side to side, her throat constricted, making speech almost impossible.

'Alicia.' His surprise was evident, but he recovered far quicker than she did, his obsidian eyes narrowing, regarding her slowly, scanning her face first—from the tip of her pale hair to her wide-set green eyes, to her curving pink lips—and then lower, to the décolletage that was exposed by the silk evening gown she wore. She'd already been a bundle of nerves—the night was the biggest charity gala she'd organised and she'd put a lot of pressure on herself to raise a small fortune. But seeing Graciano tipped her completely off balance.

'What are you doing here?' she blurted out. True, she hadn't seen a guest list for two days— once all the tickets were sold, she hadn't been particularly interested in who was coming, only that the usual high-flying donors were registered to bid in the charity auction. But she would have noticed Graciano's name on the list, which meant he was a late addition.

'Last I checked, it's a free country,' he drawled, his voice rich with authority and mockery, his accent so familiar to her that her toes curled inside her shoes. Everything inside her pinched together. This man—he was a sinkhole. He always had been. But it was so much worse than that, now. He was also the father to her daughter. Their daughter—a child he knew nothing about, because he'd made it impossible for Alicia to contact him after that one awful, heart-destroying morning in Seville.

'Did you come here to see me?' she asked, confused by his appearance after ten years. Good Lord, was it possible he knew about Annie? Had he come to confront Alicia? To take Annie away? All the heat drained from her face as the possibility of that scored deep into her heart.

'What reason could I possibly have for wanting to see you, Alicia?'

Her eyes widened at his obvious scorn, and

even when she knew she should be *glad*, because it meant he didn't know the truth, it only made her more on edge.

The last time she'd seen this man, he'd been eighteen years old—still a teenager, but with more determination in his little finger than most people had in their whole bodies. There had to be a reason for him being at the auction.

'You tell me,' she suggested, casting a quick glance over his shoulder. She needed to get towards the stage, but her feet felt almost glued to the ground.

'No reason,' he said firmly, lips compressed. 'Ten years ago, I swore you were the last person I wanted to see, and my opinion has not changed.'

She flinched at the coldness in his tone. That morning in Seville, her father's words, what he'd accused Graciano of—it was burned into her mind. How many nights had she dreamed of that, had she wished she'd done something, said something? Instead, she'd taken her father's side and watched this man be eviscerated, bullied and then sent packing. Never mind that she'd tried to apologise, to explain. That she'd tried to tell him about the child they'd conceived.

He'd removed Alicia from his life completely, and she couldn't fault him for that.

'It was a long time ago,' she said quietly, even when that wasn't really true. Annie made their past very, very relevant.

'Yes,' he agreed with a shrug. 'If you'll excuse me, my date is waiting.'

Before she could stop herself, she glanced over her shoulder to see a leggy redhead emerge from the ladies' room and swish her curling hair over one shoulder, then strut towards Graciano as though she were on a catwalk and not in a hotel ballroom corridor.

'Graciano—' Alicia said his name with a frown. What could she add? Annie was at the forefront of her mind. She'd tried to tell him, but as he'd become more and more successful, it had become impossible to contact him. Eventually, she'd given up trying and come to terms with the fact that even if she'd told him, he wouldn't have wanted anything to do with a child of Alicia's. But now? He was right in front of her. Alicia surely had an obligation to find a way to break the news to him?

And then what?

Risk a custody dispute if she'd been wrong?

With someone this rich and powerful?

'I—'

His glare was withering, his hands in his pockets a casual stance that was belied by the taut lines of his muscular frame.

'Could you meet me for a drink later?' she said softly, knowing that no matter how terrified she was of telling him, it was the right thing to do. She certainly needed to at least get to know him again now she had this opportunity, to work out what her next step should be. After all, Annie had to be her number one priority. Whatever debt she owed Graciano had been watered down by his refusal to take her calls, and then by him changing his number to be sure she got the message, loud and clear.

'No.'

His bald refusal made her stomach drop to the ground. She hadn't anticipated that.

'Give me ten minutes.'

'It is a long time since I've felt I needed to "give" you anything,' he ground out, and she knew then that the passage of time hadn't watered down his feelings at all. He was as angry with his treatment now as he had been then.

And little wonder. Her father had berated the man for nearly thirty minutes, hurling every insult in the book at him, and Alicia had stood there, silent, by her father's side, complicit in the abuse because she'd stood there and said nothing. She could still remember the look on Graciano's face as he'd turned to her. She'd known he'd been waiting for her to defend him, to explain that it hadn't been sexual assault at all, but a relationship.

And Alicia hadn't been able to bring herself to incur her father's anger. She'd put self-preservation above everything else, even Graciano.

For anyone, that would have been a deal breaker, but for a man like Graciano, who was as proud as the sun was hot, who'd been mistreated and abandoned almost all his life, her rejection had been unforgivable.

'Please.'

His eyes narrowed at the softly voiced word, and her spine tingled from the base of her head to the curve of her bottom. The redhead was almost level with them now; Alicia knew the window was closing. But if he'd come to the ball, then her assistant would have his contact information. She didn't have to do *anything* tonight.

'Never mind,' she said after a beat, shaking her head a little so a clump of smooth blond hair fell over her eyes. She lifted a hand to move it, and her skin lifted in goosebumps as his gaze followed the gesture. 'It doesn't matter.'

He dipped his head in silent agreement, and before she could say another word, he turned, placed an arm around the redhead's waist and led her deeper into the ballroom, where the festive scene was completely at odds with the churning sensation deep in Alicia's gut.

The door to her past had just cracked open, and she had no choice but to step through it.

There was not a lot that held the power to surprise Graciano Cortéz. But the truth was, ten years after being thrown out of Alicia Griffiths' home, he'd truly believed he'd never seen her again. He believed she no longer held power over him, that he was beyond her reach. He believed she was dead to him.

As she stood on the stage before him, the bolt of recognition spiking in his spine belied that—the same bolt that had almost sheared him in half in the corridor twenty minutes earlier.

A decade ago, in that brief, halcyon time of his life, he'd thought for a moment that he'd found his feet, that someone had accepted him just as he was—loved him, even. Someone had made him smile, and laugh, and trust, and all of the things he thought were dead inside of him she'd brought back to life. Not effortlessly. He'd built his protective shielding brick by brick, and he'd tried to hold on to it in the face of her attention, but little by little, she'd drawn down his guard.

Which was why that morning had been so powerfully awful.

Bitterness washed over him, as memories of his foolish mistake hammered through his brain.

You're worthless, boy, pure street scum

through and through, and you always will be.
Always. You're dead to me. Now get the hell off
my land before I call the police.

Even now, ten years later, the ugliness of that
morning had the ability to tighten the nerves in
Graciano's body, to flood his body with adrenaline and fill his mouth with a metallic taste.

At the first test of his true sentiment, Edward
had thrown Graciano out, back onto the streets,
with no care for how that rejection might impact
him. And Alicia had watched, silent, choosing to
lie to her father rather than admit that the sex had
been consensual, that they were in—no, not love.
It hadn't been that. At the time, he'd thought it
was, but he'd been a stupid, foolish teenager,
looking for something that didn't exist.

It had been hormones, lust, desire, the pleasure and temptation of the forbidden fruit, one
of the oldest seduction tools of all time. He'd
wanted her because he couldn't have her. Love
wasn't a part of it. As for Alicia, she'd thrown
him under a bus, letting her father accuse him of
rape and throw him back onto the streets. She'd
moved closer to Edward, slid her hand into the
crook of the minister's arm, making it clear that
she had no intention of speaking the truth.

She'd betrayed Graciano. He'd learned a lot
from her and her father, and ever since, he'd

kept people at arm's length as though his life depended on it.

He ground his teeth together, watching intently as she strode onto the stage, replaying their brief interaction. Her smile was self-conscious. Because of him?

Graciano tightened his grip on his knee, sitting as still as a piece of stone as she moved to the lectern.

'Good evening.' Her eyes swept the crowd. Looking for him?

That she was older was obvious. She was more sophisticated and womanly, her bearing far less mischievous than that of the sixteen-year-old he'd followed around like a puppy dog when he was, himself, only eighteen. Her hair, rather than being a tumble of coarse blonde curls that flopped wildly down her back, was still fair, but far sleeker, pulled back into an elegant ponytail that glistened as she moved her head. Her makeup was impeccable—the Alicia he'd known had never worn anything cosmetic. Her father would have never allowed it for his little girl.

Objectively, she was beautiful, but she always had been. Despite his hatred of her, Graciano had felt old feelings of desire stir in his gut that had made him want to lean forward and brush her loose hair from her face, to let his fingers drift over her cheeks. He'd wanted to touch her soft lips with his hand, then his mouth—beneath his breath, he uttered a curse.

Ten years had passed since they'd touched one another, and he'd been with enough women since then to know how to indulge his body's wants. But this was different.

He didn't simply desire Alicia.

It was darker than that.

He felt a compulsion to be with her, to remind her of what they'd shared before her father had ruined it. To make her admit it had meant something. Until that moment, he hadn't realised how much he needed that.

Her father had hurt him, yes, but it had been Alicia's rejection that had irrevocably broken something inside of him. She'd acted as though he meant nothing to her. She'd acted as though he didn't matter, and suddenly, it was the most important thing in Graciano's life to make her admit that hadn't been the case.

'Thank you all for coming.' Her voice trembled a little and he leaned forward, wondering if it was the effect of seeing him again that had unnerved her. 'This is the fourth year I've had the privilege of organising the annual McGiven House charity auction, and the first in which I'll be taking part,' she added with a wry grimace, finding her confidence as she went on. The crowd cheered loudly. She lifted her hands placatingly, effortlessly charming and modest in a way he took to be studied. After all, the rapturous response spoke of an established acceptance of the fact that she was in high demand.

He leaned ever so slightly forward in his seat, oblivious to the people at his table, including his date—who, in that moment, he couldn't even remember the name of.

'Never fear, I will *not* be your MC for the evening,' she said with a soft laugh that sent a thousand arrows firing through his skin. That laugh had brushed over him, breathing across his body, teasing him, promising him, taunting him, demanding of him, just as it always had.

Could you meet me for a drink later?

He pressed his fingers into his thigh with more strength. The invitation had blurted out of her mouth, and he'd been so tempted to agree—which was why he'd immediately, harshly, responded in the negative.

He dropped his head forward, his breath strained, and he felt his date cast him a curious look. It sobered Graciano, and he remembered an important lesson he'd learned many years ago: never reveal your feelings. Keep your cards close to your chest. Never show them how you feel.

Never let them know you're hurting.

Never let anyone see your pain.

He straightened, renewed determination in his eyes as he focused with laser-like intensity on the stage, waiting with the appearance of calm as the charity auction proceeded, many valuable items being offered to the delighted audience. The sums attained by each lot were truly eye watering, reflecting both the value of the listings as well as the worthiness of the cause: McGiven House offered respite accommodation to those fleeing domestic violence. It was a cause close to Graciano's heart—he had personally donated millions of euros to charities such as this, and yet it never felt like enough.

Until he could forget what it was like to go to bed starving and afraid, he would never feel that he'd done what was necessary.

Graciano went through the motions for the evening, making conversation where necessary, even as every cell in his body was focused on the last lot of the night—Alicia herself—and an idea began to take hold.

A foolish idea, one he knew he shouldn't credit, yet couldn't ignore.

As he watched her, so effortlessly graceful and charming, convincing everyone that her heart was made of pure gold, all he could think of was her actions towards him, of how easy she found it to see him cast out onto the street once more, of how that rejection had stung him to the core.

Graciano didn't make decisions based on emotional impulses; it wasn't wise. But in that moment, it was a thirst for revenge, a need for retaliation, that had his insides firing to life with determination. Ten years ago, she'd destroyed his trust, and even though he'd moved on and built a hell of a life for himself, the effects of her treatment had spread through his life like poisoned tentacles, and he sought—needed—an exorcism of sorts.

He wouldn't have sought her out, but given that they'd crossed paths once more, he refused to look a gift horse in the mouth.

Alicia Griffiths would be his, and he'd make her admit how wrong she'd been to discard him as though he were trash.

'Remind me why I let you talk me into this?' Alicia muttered to her assistant, casting her a pleading look as the second-to-last auction item entered a frenzied bidding war. It had been nerve-racking enough *before* she'd known Graciano was in the audience.

'Because you are altruism itself,' Connie said with a wink.

'Yes, yes, but I'm *behind-the-scenes* altruism. Auctioning myself off is madness.'

'Firstly, you're auctioning your considerable experience as an events planner, not yourself.

Secondly, it's far too late to back out. I happen to know Maude Peterson is desperate to secure you for her granddaughter's wedding and has her chequebook at the ready.'

Alicia raised a single brow, but she was distracted. 'A wedding, hmm?' That would require her to put aside her innate disbelief in the idea of *happily ever after*—or at least, pretend to.

'A very expensive English country wedding with a list of well-heeled guests who would all be excellent donors to our charity,' Connie pointed out, bringing Alicia's attention back to the current scenario.

'I don't think I can tout for donations at a wedding.'

'No, but Maude is a gossip and she's bound to tell everyone about the charity.'

'Yes, that's true.' Alicia pulled her lips to one side, eyes skimming the audience as her stomach flipped and flopped. Just the idea that Graciano was there, that he'd be watching her, made her feel a thousand kinds of strange.

Butterflies filled her belly as the auctioneer raised his gavel. Her eyes flitted to the screen behind him, blinking with surprise at the huge amount the first-class trip to New York—donated by a footballer—had achieved. Well above the ticket price, but of course, it wasn't just flights and premier accommodation: the internationally famous sports star had offered to cook dinner for the winners and host them in his home—a truly generous donation. Everyone was doing their bit, and now it was Alicia's turn.

Besides, taking a week of annual leave and using it to plan an event for some rich socialite was hardly arduous. She could plan any event in her sleep, and it would be nice to turn her skills to something other than charity dinners, fun runs and auctions.

The auctioneer began to introduce Alicia, reading the bio Connie had provided:

'Alicia Griffiths is a name known to all of us for her tireless work at McGiven House. Since joining the organisation four years ago, she's more than trebled the charity's income and raised the profile, enabling us to expand our offerings fourfold. In practical terms, that means we help a lot more people because she's put us in a position to do so. Prior to joining McGiven House, Alicia worked for the Royal Family as a protocol and events officer, and now, her pedigree and skills as an event planner are available to you. Alicia is generously offering one week of her time to arrange whatever event you have in mind. Be it corporate or personal, her work will be limited only by your imagination.'

The auctioneer turned to the side of the ballroom, where Alicia continued to wait in the wings. 'Alicia? Join me on stage.'

Her stomach was in a thousand knots and her knees were shaking. He was out there somewhere; that derisive curl of his lips haunted her as she walked on stage.

'You're sure I can't back out?' she muttered to Connie, only half joking as she took a step onto the stage.

'I'm sure.' Connie gave her a gentle nudge, pushing her the rest of the way. Alicia crossed to the auctioneer's side, glad that it was impossible to see out into the crowd because her nerves wouldn't have stood the idea of all those eyes staring back at her.

'Shall we start the bidding at ten thousand pounds?'

What if no one bid on her? And Graciano was there to witness her embarrassment.

'Ten thousand pounds!' She recognised Maude's voice and dipped her head forward in a smile. The wedding was clearly very special to the older woman. For a moment, Alicia felt a familiar pang, the same aching sense of longing whenever she was confronted with the love one family member had for another. How nice it must be to have someone prepared to fight your fights! But Alicia, in the end, had fought her own—was still fighting them, in fact. Being a single mother, even to a wonderful little girl, wasn't a walk in the park.

'Ten thousand pounds,' the auctioneer said after a brief pause that denoted surprise. He leaned forward on the lectern. 'Do I have fifteen?'

'Fifteen!' Another voice—a woman, but not instantly familiar to Alicia—entered the fray.

Before the auctioneer could respond, Maude chimed in. 'Twenty!'

Then another voice, male this time, and older. 'Twenty-five.'

Alicia turned towards Connie, her face a study in surprise. This had not been anticipated.

'Thirty!' Maude again. She really was determined.

'Thirty-five.' The other female voice.

'Fifty!' Maude shouted, and Alicia could just imagine the woman's determined expression.

'I have fifty thousand pounds for one week of Alicia's time.'

Alicia dug her fingernails into her palm. She was going to have to pull out all the stops for this bloody wedding: doves, rainbows, magic. It would have to be perfect.

Keeping a smile plastered on her face, with her heart beating so loud it filled her ears, she scanned the room. The lights were too bright to see clearly, but she knew he was out there, and it set fire to every nerve ending in her body.

'Fifty thousand pounds going once.' The auctioneer paused dramatically—and without any real need. No way would anyone spend more than that for an events planner. 'Going twice.'

Alicia held her breath with the rest of the crowd. There was total silence. She waited for the gavel to drop, desperate for this to be over so she could scurry offstage, but in the seconds before, as the auctioneer lifted it, a voice rang out, clear and gruff, accented and immediately impactful, sending something inside Alicia rioting on a tumble of uncertainty.

'Five hundred thousand pounds.'

The silence gave way to murmurs of shock and Alicia lifted a hand to her lips. She recognised the voice instantly. Her heart leaped into her throat and she turned to the auctioneer, who was beaming with pleasure.

'Just to be sure I didn't mishear...was that five hundred thousand pounds?'

'Yes.'

Alicia stood there, in the middle of a world that had begun to spin far too fast on its axis. 'A generous offer indeed! Are you a registered bidder, sir?'

Alicia leaned closer once more and spoke au-

tomatically, her voice heavy with emotion. 'All
ticket holders are pre-registered to bid.'

The auctioneer covered the microphone. 'Then
it's binding.'

Alicia turned to face the crowd, her lips parted
with shock. Silently, she pleaded with Graciano, wherever he was, to rethink this. But it was
too late. Such a generous offer was going to be
snapped up by the auctioneer, who rushed to
drop the gavel. Alicia flinched, eyes huge as she
stared out at the crowd.

'Ladies and gentlemen, what a truly exceptional evening. Those of you lucky enough to
secure an item, or person—' he turned to Alicia and grinned '—please leave your details and
payment at the administration booth near the
door within the hour. Collection will be arranged
Monday morning.'

Alicia waited by the administration desk with
nerves that wouldn't calm down. Five hundred
thousand pounds? What on earth had he been
thinking?

She paced behind the desk as other winners
came and signed contracts, obligating them to
make payment for their items, or left cheques,
all of which Connie would oversee in the office Monday morning. She waited and her eyes
skimmed the crowd—more visible now the

lights had softened—looking for Graciano. Maybe she could get him to change his mind?

But the idea of losing that money for the charity tightened around her throat like a noose. She couldn't do that.

'This is a mistake,' she said to Connie as she stalked behind the table. 'I can't… This is… We should approach Maude and see if she's still happy to pay—'

'That will not be necessary.'

With her back to the room, Alicia froze, all the colour and warmth draining from her face as his voice wrapped around her, strangling her, shocking her, so her heart felt as though it had been electrocuted.

'Connie.' It was a strangled plea, but for what? What did she want her assistant to say or do?

'Good evening, sir. Are you the lucky winner of Miss Griffiths' services?'

She barely heard Connie's question. Her ears were ringing and her mind was in free fall at the realisation that not only Graciano was here, but that he'd *bid* on her.

'Yes.'

'Wonderful. And what was your name, sir?'

Alicia turned slowly, bracing herself to come face to face with him again, this time with the knowledge he'd just pledged an exorbitant amount for a week of her time.

'This is Graciano Cortéz, Connie,' Alicia said quietly.

A thousand billion feelings slammed into her like an out-of-control train.

Her face was ashen, her eyes haunted when they met his, but only for a moment. She rallied quickly, imposing a cool mask to her features, but oh, how it cost her. What was he thinking? He'd swiftly declined even the idea of a drink, of ten minutes of shared airspace, and yet he'd bid an outrageous amount on her event-organising skills?

'Someone you know?' Connie asked.

She was quick to dispute that. 'Just someone I spent time with many years ago.' It felt important to delineate the past from their present. She ignored the mockery that shifted on his face, a mockery she immediately understood, because she understood *everything* about Graciano Cortéz, and probably always would.

'I see.' Connie frowned.

Alicia infused a note of disdain into her voice; after all, what more did he deserve? 'I take it you have an event you'd like me to organise?'

His eyes narrowed almost imperceptibly. 'Correct.'

'I see. Well, if you leave your details with my assistant, Connie, I'll be in touch once the payment has cleared.'

'I'll require you to start Monday.'

'Monday?' Alicia stared at him, momentarily forgetting she was supposed to be unflappable. 'Why so soon?'

'The event is at the end of the month.'

'How come you haven't arranged it already?'

'I wasn't aware my five hundred thousand pounds also bought me an inquisition. Can you do it, or not?'

Alicia shot Connie a look of disbelief and Connie's own features reflected bemusement. 'You have two meetings, but I can move them back a week…'

It was not the answer Alicia wanted.

'What is your name?' Graciano's attention shifted to Alicia's right.

'Connie.'

'My assistant will send an itinerary to you tomorrow morning, Connie. I will require Ms Griffiths' services for five nights. Her flight will leave first thing Monday morning.'

'Hold on a second.' Alicia needed to draw breath. For a moment, she was sixteen again, all her hopes and wants and dreams centred around this man, and the reality of how far life had taken her from him, of how far from one another they were now, almost made her physically ill. Would her sixteen-year-old self ever have understood that they could speak so coldly to one another?

For a time, he'd truly felt like the other part of her. But it had just been a childish dream, nothing more. 'A week of my time means a week of my time, not... I can't... You're not seriously expecting me to go to Spain with you?'

'I presume my five hundred thousand pounds buys me your undivided attention?'

'Well, yes, but I can give you that from my office at home—'

'No.' He responded coldly, but with obvious determination. 'The event is to take place on my island, and so, too, should the planning. You cannot possibly arrange what is necessary without seeing the place for yourself. If you want my money, accept these terms.'

Her jaw dropped.

'Mr Cortéz.' Connie tried to imbue a little formality back into the conversation. 'That is not the way these things usually—'

'My donation is not usual,' he said with the confidence of a man who was completely right. 'This is the deal. Take it or leave it.'

Every fibre of Alicia's body willed her to reject it—to tell him to go to hell. A week on Graciano's island? She wasn't crazy. She wasn't stupid. But she'd already tabulated what his half a million pounds could do—how many families it could help. There was no way she'd be the reason the charity lost his donation. Bitterness crept through her as she mentally moved the pieces of her life around. Diane would have Annie. Her schedule was hectic, even though she was only working part-time now—she volunteered extensively, and had a wide social circle. But Alicia knew she only had to ask and Diane would help. The older woman had become like a mother or grandmother to Alicia, the one person in her life she had been able to rely on since Annie was still growing inside of her.

It would be a wrench to be away from her daughter for five nights—they'd never been separated for more than a night, and even then only rarely and when necessary—but Annie was no longer a baby. At nine years old, she felt on the cusp of becoming a teenager already, her legs growing impossibly long and slim, her hair falling all the way to her waist, wild like Alicia's always had been, but chestnut brown rather than sunlight blonde.

Annie no longer pined for Alicia, calling for her in the middle of the night. She was a confident, well-liked girl who adored school and spoke with the maturity of a much older child. She would cope without Alicia for a week.

A pang of hurt resonated in Alicia's heart, even when she knew that independence was a good thing, really. It still felt like a betrayal of sorts.

She watched as Graciano reached into his pocket and withdrew his phone. 'I'll wire the money now, if I have your agreement.'

How on earth did he become so ridiculously wealthy?

An image of him on that last day formed in her mind, as clear as if it were a photograph: scruffy running shoes, old jeans, a loose T-shirt. Her throat ached. Even with his second-hand clothes, he'd always carried himself with confidence and class. He'd always been destined for more than the life he'd found himself living. The question wasn't how he'd made his fortune, but why she'd ever doubted him.

'Alicia?' Connie frowned at her boss, obviously picking up on Alicia's ambivalence and hesitating in response.

Alicia stared at Graciano, wishing she understood him as well now as she had then. What was he thinking? What did he want?

'It's a very generous donation, Mr Cortéz.' She deliberately kept them on a more business-like footing, but his lip curled with a hint of derision—lips that had dragged over her body, tasted her most intimate flesh, teased her breasts, left purple circles on her skin from where he'd sucked her until she'd cried out. Heat flushed her face and she looked away quickly. 'Connie will handle the formalities. If you'll excuse me, there's someone I have to speak to.'

'You're really going to Spain? For a week?'

It was impossible to meet Annie's intelligent, inquisitive eyes. A new kind of guilt, most unsavoury, flooded Alicia, to look at the little girl who was so like the father she'd never met—the father who'd made it clear he didn't want to hear from Alicia ever again.

Until last night.

She was baffled and she was terrified in equal measure as choices she'd made as a scared, abandoned sixteen-year-old were suddenly raised to the light, making her question everything she'd once chosen.

She'd *tried* to tell him, she reminded herself. She hadn't wanted this. She hadn't chosen this. Nonetheless, the fact she had borne Graciano's baby and raised her for nine years suddenly felt like a crime.

'Mummy?'

Mummy. Alicia's heart clutched. Not such a pre-teen yet, then.

Tears lodged in her throat as she made herself look into her beloved daughter's eyes directly. She was all tucked up in her still very childish bed, in the small pale pink room at the top of the stairs.

'Well, darling, it's supposed to be five nights, but I'm going to try my hardest to get home sooner. Do you think you'll be okay?'

Annie wrinkled her nose, snuggling deeper into the pillows. 'You do know Didee lets me eat ice cream *before* dinner when you're not here.'

Alicia laughed. 'Is that why we never seem to have any left in the freezer when I go looking?'

'No, that's because Didee has two huge bowls all to herself,' Annie corrected, and Alicia's heart panged. 'What's Spain like?'

Visions of sunshine flooded her thoughts, of oranges picked straight from the tree and eaten while still warm, crystal clear water, rolling hills, clay buildings, music that breathed life into your soul, the kindest people in the world... Graciano when he'd first arrived, all skin and bone with angry, dark eyes and fascinating, capable hands, so silent at first, so cold, that she couldn't help but want to make him smile.

'It's beautiful.' Her voice was croaky.

'How long did you live there?'

'Five years.' She cleared her throat. 'We moved right after your grandmother—my mother—passed away.'

'Where exactly?'

'Your grandfather had a property outside of Seville, and a church on the edge of the city.' The mission had been attached to the church, caring for homeless kids, of which there'd been a large number.

'Will you go to Seville?'

'Not on this trip.'

'Will you see your father?'

Anger flattened Alicia's lips but she avoided expressing it to her daughter. 'No, darling. I don't think so.' She'd been careful not to colour Annie's opinions of the minister, but as the little girl grew older, she had naturally shown more curiosity. One day, Alicia would have to be honest about the rift that had formed between them, about the way her father had thrown her away, so disappointed in her for becoming pregnant at sixteen that he hadn't been able to continue living with her.

You are my greatest failure, Alicia.

One day, she'd tell her daughter that Edward Griffiths, admired and respected man of faith, had threatened to press charges against Graciano if Alicia ever spoke to him again. That threat had hung over her head for years. As a girl, she'd believed it unfailingly, and even now, as an adult, she credited the cynical likelihood of Edward's words.

That boy from the streets, with no family and no one to speak for him, took advantage of you in my *home. No police officer or judge is going to believe him. He will rot in jail for this. Just give me the excuse to do it and I will. He deserves it.*

'Why not?'

She was dragged back to the present, her palms sweaty, her heart quickening.

'I'm going for work, and I'm not going to waste a moment doing anything other than work, because I'll be so desperate to come home to you.' She leaned forward and pressed a kiss to Annie's forehead. 'Di will pick you up from school tomorrow,' she said. 'And I'll see you Saturday morning for football, okay?'

'We're playing Ridgehaven.'

'I know.' Alicia smiled, standing, doing her best to hide the distracting direction of her thoughts.

'They're really good.'

'Yes, but so are you.' She tousled her little girl's vanilla-scented hair. 'Go to sleep, darling. I'll see you in the morning.'

Graciano's eyes chased the rolling waves as though he could find meaning in their rhythm, as though the depths of the sea might help him gain clarity, but there was none. He stared at the sea, all the questions that usually plagued him swirling and churning—and central to those questions was where was his brother? He thought again of yet another thwarted lead, of hopes raised then dashed, of the compounding certainty that he was all alone on this earth, his entire family lost to him forever.

He'd come to accept that reality.

But seeing Alicia again had stirred everything up, had made him remember a time when he'd hoped for a new family, when his heart had begun to crack open, just a little.

Only for it to slam shut in spectacular fashion, never to be opened again.

The decision to invent a function for her to organise had been spontaneous and immediate, yet he didn't regret it. Graciano trusted his instincts, and the moment he saw her again, he'd known it was long past time for her to reckon with how she'd treated him.

Lately, he'd been thinking of his brother again. Of his parents. Of a childhood that shimmered on his horizon like blades of sunshine—ephemeral and striking, warm and impossible to grab hold of. His mother's laugh, his father's voice, his brother's little body, his hand slipping into Graciano's to hold as they crossed the road, walking to school.

He'd been loved, and he had loved deeply, and then he'd lost, in the most horrific of circumstances. He could vividly recall the sound of metal on metal as their car was hit and pushed into the railing on the side of the road.

He closed his eyes, pushing those thoughts away, ignoring the throbbing feeling deep in his gut, a yearning for something he'd lost long ago that could never be replaced.

Graciano was a pragmatist. He couldn't get his brother back, he couldn't save his parents and he couldn't find his way back to his family, but he had all the money in the world, and on this one occasion, he could use it to right at least one wrong of his past: he could make Alicia eat crow, and that was a delight he intended to savour…

CHAPTER TWO

IT WAS A RELIEF, Alicia told herself, that Graciano hadn't appeared at London City Airport to meet her on Monday morning. It was also a relief that he hadn't been onboard the extremely luxurious private jet that had carried her from London to an airstrip in Valencia, and from there to a sleek, white helicopter that had lifted up over the Balearic Sea, conveying Alicia the short distance from mainland Spain to a cluster of islands a little to the east of the city.

The helicopter circled the cluster before moving closer to one, the largest of six, something that from the air, at first glance, looked like a place that time had forgotten. The forest was so verdant and sprawling it seemed almost prehistoric, but as the helicopter came in lower and offered a different vantage point, she saw that the western side of the island was more developed. A golf course was unmistakable, as well as a large, white-walled mansion with a central courtyard bursting with colourful vines, and several smaller buildings dotted away from the main house but joined to it via paved roads. Lower still they came, and she saw a fleet of golf buggies, some parked at the smaller cottages, others lined up on the side of the mansion. The beach was immaculate, all white sand and clear sea, and there were two swimming pools—one beside the house, and a smaller one surrounded by colourful trees and vines, but most inviting of all on a warm day like this was the ocean that glittered with the force of diamonds, making her ache to wade out to hip height, then dive beneath the surface.

How long had it been since she'd had a holiday?

Any kind of holiday?

She'd taken Annie to Cornwall when she was four, just for a weekend, but it had been perfect. They'd eaten ice cream and bought fish and chips, which they'd shared with dozens of hungry—or plain greedy—seagulls, and walked through narrow, cobbled lanes while smiling at locals. But it had been short, and hardly exotic. This, though, was not a holiday, despite the picturesque location.

Not only was this a work trip, but she couldn't afford to forget that fact for even one moment. She had no idea why Graciano had done this, but there was no forgetting their past, and she couldn't ever relax around him.

The issue of their daughter was an ever-present nightmare, a ticking time bomb she knew

she would have to face head-on, but had no idea
how to.

The helicopter touched down on a paved cir-
cular area joined to the house by a path lined
on either side with espaliered fruit trees. Graciano stood in the centre of the path, feet planted
wide and arms crossed over his chest, his body
language anything but welcoming. In fact, if he
hadn't paid so much money for her expertise,
and insisted on her coming to this island, she'd
have said he was resenting her presence.

Well, that made two of them.

From the confines of the helicopter, she took
a moment to observe him without being observed. Time had changed both of them, though
she feared it had been much kinder to him. As
an eighteen-year-old, Graciano had been slender—far too slender, courtesy of his life on the
streets and too many skipped meals. He'd always
been hypermasculine despite that, with a raw
virility and confidence, but this was something
else. His six-and-a-half-foot frame had filled out,
so he stood muscular and strong, every inch of
him conveying pure alpha male dominance. She
knew enough about men's clothes to know that
those he wore were the very best, though they
weren't visibly branded. Their quality was obvious. He didn't go to any effort with his appearance; he was too much of a man's man for that,

too focused on other things, but that didn't matter. Effort or not, he was, without a doubt, the most beautiful person she'd ever seen.

His face was remarkable.

It always had been.

Her heart leaped into her throat as she remembered the first day they'd met. A summer storm had crossed Seville. She'd been terrified of the lightning, and from her reading spot in the conservatory, it was louder and brighter than anywhere else in the house, only she couldn't get inside without crossing through the garden. Graciano had been working, pruning fruit trees, when he'd heard her scream. He'd told her later that it had chilled his blood. He'd thrown open the door and lightning had crashed behind him, but she was no longer afraid. She hadn't even seen it.

All of her had become focused on all of him.

He'd worn a singlet top and shorts that sat low on his hips, and his shoes had been old and saturated. But none of that had mattered. She was transfixed by him. His jaw was square, as if chiselled from stone, his cheekbones angular and sharp. Stubble covered his chin, and his eyes were the darkest brown she'd ever seen, rimmed in thick, black lashes that were made even more dramatic by the falling rain. His hair had become drenched, but he'd driven his hands through it, pushing it back from his face, which had only served to draw attention to his high, fascinating brow.

'Who are you?' she'd gasped, lifting a hand to her chest.

'Graciano. Are you hurt?'

It was so like him. He'd brushed aside the fact they didn't know one another and had concentrated only on the information he'd wanted. He'd taken control, even then, as a street kid with nothing and no one.

He was Graciano. All hail Graciano.

As he stood there now, she felt the same power emanating off him, the same unfaltering command of a situation, and she knew she had to do a better job of guarding against those feelings this time, or she'd be as fully under his spell as she had been back then.

The thought terrified her into action.

She unclipped her seatbelt and moved to the central door of the cabin, so that the moment it was opened and the stairs brought down she could disembark, in control and ready for business. To prove that point, she pulled her handbag over one shoulder, taking comfort from the weight of her laptop and notebook. Only at that exact moment, her eyes sought, of their own accord, Graciano, and the manoeuvre of pulling her strap threw her off balance, so that as she took the second step, her ankle twisted and rolled. She extended an arm on autopilot, her hand curling around the railing for a vital second before slipping, her knees crumbling. She righted herself, somehow, for another excruciating second, but the momentum was too great.

She tumbled to the ground and lay, splayed like roadkill, on the elegant herringbone red brick pavers.

'Great,' she muttered under her breath, the sting in her scraped knees nothing to the monumental hole in her pride. 'Just bloody great.'

To Alicia, it felt like a lifetime, but in reality, it took Graciano mere seconds to reach her. First, she heard his feet, not running, but walking with speed, and stopping right by her head, so she was greeted with obviously hand-stitched leather boots right in front of her face.

'Alicia.' He drawled her name with that awful cynicism of his.

Ignoring his proffered hand, cheeks flaming, she pushed up gingerly, her knees complaining as she moved, so she curled one hand around the railing and dragged herself halfway to standing before her ankle gave an almighty shot of pain and she let out a groaning sound, angry eyes piercing Graciano, as though he had somehow manipulated these circumstances.

'What is it?' he demanded again, and now,

to her absolute chagrin, he put a hand around her back, steadying her, or at least, intending to steady her, but in reality it had the opposite effect, as a thousand blades shot through her body at his simple, light touch. His fingers splayed wide, forming a barrier over her hip. The movement somehow so intimate and familiar, and she was far too aware of him.

'Don't,' she hissed, pulling away from him, then yelping again when her ankle almost rolled once more. 'I've twisted my ankle,' she snapped, as though it were his fault.

'Evidently.'

'I saw a heap of golf carts when we were flying over. Maybe one of those could help me to the house?'

'That's not necessary.' Before she could intuit his meaning, he caught her around the waist and lifted her, cradling her against his chest as though she weighed nothing. It was an overwhelming moment. Ten years ago, they'd been lovers, but only once, only one night, and since then, they hadn't seen each other. She hadn't been touched by anyone. She'd been flirted with, asked out on dates, but no one had elicited a single frisson of warmth from her, let alone a full-blown fire.

Why the hell was it like this with them? Why

did his touch send her nerves skittling all over the place?

She startled against his body, aware of every movement of his muscles, aware of his masculine fragrance, the stubble on his jaw.

'I'm sure I can walk,' she lied, earning a look of cynical mockery from him.

'Do you want me to put you down so you can try?'

He'd called her bluff, and damn it, they both knew the answer to that. Even if she hadn't found being in his arms powerfully addictive, her ankle couldn't possibly support her weight in that moment.

She didn't answer, focusing her gaze on the house in front of them instead. There was plenty to look at, and even more as they drew nearer to it. From the sky, it had been beautiful, but on the ground level, she could observe and appreciate many more features, like the windows that were carved into the walls, each boasting a terracotta window box overflowing with geraniums and sweet peas.

'It's stunning,' she said, before she could stop herself.

He walked slowly, each step long and confident, but the house felt like it was miles away. Each step bumped her against his chest, so her body was aware of him on a cellular level. She wanted this to end, she told herself forcefully, even when a part of her—a very small part—was transfixed by the power of this moment, by the strangest sense in the world that being in his arms was like…coming home.

As she'd noticed from the air, the house was square in shape, with a large central courtyard. When Graciano stepped through the double-width blue wooden door into a tiled hallway, she caught glimpses of the courtyard and almost swooned. She put it at the top of her list for further investigation, once her ankle permitted. The rooms were large with high ceilings. He carried her through the entrance way and into a living room with Moroccan-style tiles on the floor, a tapestry on the wall and mid-century lounges. It was an eclectic, stylish mix of furniture that she put down to an interior designer's eye rather than Graciano's.

When he reached the sofa, he placed her down onto it, releasing her immediately so she wanted to cry out at the desertion of his touch, but she tamped down on that instinct forcefully.

She'd fallen for this man once before; no way would she let their physical chemistry tempt her again. Things between them were too complicated to allow for any personal desire. Annie had to be her priority—working out how to deal with the fact they shared a daughter he knew nothing about.

With a mutinous expression, she nodded stiffly. 'Thank you.'

Surprisingly, he laughed, a sound that made her blood simmer. 'You sound as though you'd rather tell me to go to hell than thank me.'

She ground her teeth together. 'Can't they both be true?'

'Touché.'

'Why have you brought me here?' she asked, cutting to the chase. It was hard to have the high ground she'd sought from where she lay on the sofa, but it wasn't going to stop her from seeking to take control.

'You need to rest your ankle,' he pointed out, either accidentally or purposely mistaking her question. 'Stay here while I get some ice.'

'I'm fine,' she lied, waiting until he'd strode from the room before pulling up the hem of her trouser. She was relieved to see her ankle looked normal size, with no swelling that might indicate a sprain or a break. But when she thrust it over the edge of the sofa and tested her weight on it, the joint gave a sharp burst of pain.

Damn.

She lay back and stared at the ceiling before turning her head towards the windows that framed a picture-perfect view of the Mediterranean garden in the foreground and the glistening ocean just behind. It was a perfect day, sunny and warm, summer's pleasure all around her—except there was no pleasure here, just bitterness and danger, as the secret she'd held close to her chest for ten years was now something she was being forced to grapple with.

She'd had the luxury of pretending for the past decade. Pretending he didn't exist, pretending he'd forgotten all about her, pretending this was for the best. Pretending Annie didn't need to know about her father, that she was better off without him.

It was far easier to accept those sentiments when Graciano was an absent, abstract concept, rather than a flesh-and-blood man occupying the same space as her.

Given what had happened between them, and how it had ended, she knew she'd made the only decisions she could at the time, that she'd done what was necessary to give Annie a stable, steady home. She'd always done her best for Annie.

But that didn't negate Graciano's rights.

It didn't absolve her of guilt.

And being here with him threw all that in her face, so she wanted to close her eyes and weep.

He entered the room quickly, a linen tea towel in his hand. She half expected him to hand it to her, but instead he came to her side, bending to one knee as he moved a hand over the affected ankle. Only then did he pause, a moment, before touching her, before lifting the fabric of her trouser just as she'd done—only this time, a thousand sparks ignited in her bloodstream.

'It looks fine,' he said gruffly.

'Well, it doesn't feel it,' she said with a tilt of her chin.

His eyes shifted to hers and then returned to her ankle, his hand resting there, his fingers pressing against her skin. Slowly, he pressed his fingers deeper, his inspection clinical and swift, checking for breaks, but that didn't stop Alicia's pulse from exploding in her veins.

Her mouth was dry, making speech almost impossible.

'It does not seem broken.'

'No.' The word emerged as a husky plea.

'You must rest it.'

So much for taking control. Graciano issued the command and she felt her body immediately obeying. The touch of ice against her skin was an unwelcome change—she wanted Graciano's hands back. The realisation terrified her.

She had to get a grip.

'Why don't you tell me about the event you want me to organise?'

He stood, turning his back to her, walking

towards the window, silent for several beats of time, so she asked, quietly, 'Graciano?'

'It's business,' he said, quickly. 'To mark a merger. Nothing too big—around one hundred people. Food, drinks, music. You know the sort of thing.'

She frowned. The details were a little scant for an event that was only a month away. 'Are you imagining people will stay on the island?'

'I haven't imagined anything.' He turned to face her, his eyes hooded, revealing nothing. 'That's why I bought you.'

'My services,' she corrected, mouth parched.

He dipped his head once in what she took as a nod. 'I'd like to see some concepts from you by Wednesday. I'll let you know which I like, and then you can get organising.'

'You have a lot of confidence in my abilities.'

'Why do you say that?'

'To be able to organise something suitable for your purposes in two days...'

'I do have confidence in your abilities,' he said after a moment. 'Your reputation precedes you.'

Pleasure zinged across her spine. 'How do you know about my reputation?'

'The charity auction,' he said with a casual shrug. 'The guests at my table spoke highly of you.'

'I see.' So he hadn't kept tabs on her.

Of *course* he hadn't, and for that, she should have been immeasurably glad. If he'd done *any* looking into her over the years, he'd have known about Annie. And knowing about Annie would have led to him seeing a picture of her, and then it would have been impossible to ignore the connection.

A frown marred her beautiful face at the thought of that. She'd *wanted* him to know about Annie, at first. But then, years had passed and it had been impossible to imagine Annie as anyone's but hers, to imagine her life expanding to include Graciano. He deserved to be in Annie's life, but he'd made that impossible. This was his fault, not Alicia's. But that didn't mean the situation wasn't fraught. It didn't mean she could continue to ignore their connection now that they were here, on his beautiful island, and the opportunity to confide in him was ever present.

But what if that was the wrong choice for Annie? After all, what did she know about the man Graciano had become? Not enough to embroil him in Annie's life without a little thought and planning, without doing some…research. She owed her daughter that much. The thought of spending a week with Graciano had terrified her, but maybe it was an opportunity. To get to know the man he'd grown into, and ascertain what role he could play in Annie's life. As for the buzzing she felt whenever he came close to touching her, she'd simply have to ignore it.

Alicia stared at the window, eyes intent on a single tree while she forced her breathing back to slow and rhythmic.

'You are renowned for the events you manage.'

For ten years, she'd been almost able to push the thought of Graciano's paternity from her mind, but now, it was staring her in the face, an obligation she could no longer outrun. Her reply emerged a little strained. 'Thank you.'

'I was not flattering you, so much as stating a fact. I grew my business by capitalising on people's strengths. I need an event organised in a hurry. You're capable of making it brilliant.'

'And so you paid five hundred thousand pounds,' she said with a shake of her head. 'That doesn't make sense. Any number of event companies would have—'

'None were available on short notice.'

So he'd tried booking elsewhere? That deflated her contentment a little.

'Why is it short notice?'

'The merger talks are moving more quickly than anticipated. The contracts will be signed this week and the legalities should complete within a fortnight or so.'

'And why a party?' she prompted. 'Is that

something you do every time you acquire a company? If so, I should imagine you'd have an events coordinator on staff.'

'Meaning?'

'Only that you buy so many businesses, it would make sense.'

'And how do you know what businesses I acquire?'

Heat flamed her cheeks as her guilty secret—how often she googled him—flooded her. 'You think you're the only one whose reputation precedes them? Or do you believe I'd come to a meeting in the middle of nowhere with a man I barely know without doing at least a hint of research?'

'With a man you barely know? That's not how I would categorise our relationship.'

'No?' She responded breathlessly, leaning forward a little until her ankle gave a dull throb of pain and she was forced to stay exactly where she was. 'Then how would you describe this?'

'Not having seen each other for many years does not change how well we know each other. How well we understand each other.'

She bit down on her lip. 'It was a long time ago.'

'And a lot has happened since,' he agreed, moving closer, eyes boring into hers, probing her, reading her. 'But have you ever forgotten?'

She gasped, the question lancing her with its directness, with its importance. 'Graciano—'

How could she answer? Danger surrounded her.

Think of Annie!

She had to do what was right for their daughter.

'You taught me so many lessons, Alicia, I have found it impossible to forget you.'

Her heart was beating so hard and fast it was all she could hear in her ears. 'What lessons?'

'How self-serving people can be, for starters. Even the beautiful, sweet-seeming ones.' He brushed his thumb over her jaw. 'Perhaps them most of all.'

She shivered, wrenching her face away, angered that even then, when his manner was derisive, his touch remained incendiary. 'What about me was self-serving?'

'Your silence, for one thing.'

She squeezed her eyes shut, because he was right. She'd listened to her father turn on Graciano and eviscerate him, to threaten to call the police and press charges for sexual assault, listened to her father ripping shreds off the man she'd loved, and she'd said nothing. She'd been mute, struck silent by the awful, mortifying position she'd found herself in. But then, when her father had threatened to go to the police if she ever contacted Graciano again, she'd closed off her heart, knowing she had to protect the man from the awful crime her father wanted to hang around his neck. Only when it had been imperative to speak to him had she taken that risk—not for herself, not because she'd missed him with all of herself, but because he'd had a right to know they'd made a baby. And deep down, because she'd believed he would be able to fix everything. Her heart strangled to remember the confused, terrified teenager she'd been then.

'Not everyone is as strong as you,' she said after a long, pained pause. 'My father was all I had—'

If anything, that seemed to make Graciano angrier. He made a dark sound of frustration and moved closer, crouching down beside her so their eyes were level.

'Your father accused me of raping you,' he reminded her, and the anguish in the depths of his eyes took her breath away. The accusation still had the power to hurt him. And little wonder! 'You said nothing to correct him. You let him think that of me.'

Shame sucked all the life from her cheeks. 'I told him the truth later. Afterwards.'

His eyes narrowed. Sceptically? 'Not that morning—not when it mattered.'

She shook her head slowly. 'He was so angry.'

'He had no right. We knew what we were doing.'

'We were little more than children.'

'So? What does that mean? Do you believe we made a mistake?'

How could she agree to that when Annie was the result? And even if there'd been no Annie, Alicia couldn't bring herself to regret anything about that night; it was only the morning she had wished, many times, to change.

He didn't wait for her to answer. Good, because she couldn't, anyway.

'I know you never thought I was good enough.'

She shook her head angrily. 'That's *not* true.'

'Just like your father, you were looking for a project.'

'Stop it,' she ground out, conscious of the hurt of his insults but also the closeness of his face. Of their own volition, her eyes dropped to his mouth, glorying in the outline of his lips even as she wanted to shove him backwards. How satisfying it would be to send him straight onto his butt.

'You are someone who looks to feel worthy by "helping" those less fortunate.'

'Is there something wrong?'

He ignored her interjection. 'That's what you were doing that summer, wasn't it?'

'It was ten years ago,' she said quietly, her

heart splintering. She tried to stay focused on Annie, to remain calm in the face of his anger. 'Why does it matter?'

But it did matter. A decade might have passed but the pain of their parting was as much a part of her now as it had been then. She tried to blink away from him but her eyes felt trapped.

'True. And so much has happened since.' He lifted a finger, pressing it to her cheek, and she trembled, desire making her pulse frantic. 'We're different people now.'

They were. Ten years, nine of them spent sole parenting, almost completely on her own. Alicia was not the impressionable teenager who'd fallen in love with this man the moment she'd laid eyes on him.

'But that night, the pleasure you felt, that was real, wasn't it, Alicia?' He said her name how he used to, heavy with his Spanish accent, loaded with desire. Her skin lifted in goosebumps and she shuddered, desire making it impossible to think of or feel anything else.

He leaned closer, his mouth just an inch from hers.

'Do you remember when we first kissed?'

Her heart kicked up a notch. 'No,' she muttered.

His lips showed he saw that for the lie it was. 'It was in the library. You told me you needed help fetching a book that was on the top shelf. I retrieved it, and when I handed it to you, our fingers touched and you made a soft little gasp, before lifting up and looking at me, just as you are now, silently begging me to kiss you. Do you remember that?'

She shook her head, but to which question, to which assertion?

'You snapped your fingers and I came running.'

She frowned. He wasn't wrong. Graciano had always been there for her. Anytime she'd needed him, she'd only had to ask and he'd done whatever she required. But he was mischaracterising it, taking what she'd believed to be loyalty and…friendship…and turning it into something sinister and manipulative.

'You're acting as though what happened between us was a big deal,' she said, when she could trust herself to speak again. 'But *you* were the one who left without a backwards glance. You were the one who told me, in no uncertain terms, that you'd moved on with your life, to never call you again. You were the one who changed your number.'

'I did not change my number to avoid you,' he said.

'No, I'm sure by then you'd forgotten all about me.'

'Yes. But not the lessons you taught me.'

It stung as though she'd been whipped. 'If you'd truly forgotten about me, then why does it seem as though you hate me?'

A muscle throbbed at the base of his jaw, drawing her attention to it. 'I hate people like you, like your father—'

She flinched at that. 'You don't know me.'

'I know all I need to know.'

She swept her eyes shut, fighting a tsunami of pain that was unexpectedly strong. 'Then why hire me? And don't lie to me. This isn't because you need an event planned in a hurry.'

'Why can't it be both?' He lifted a hand slowly, as though trying to fight himself, to her ear, cradling it lightly. Sparks ignited. She swallowed hard, but moved closer, even when that brought them nose to nose.

'Both what?' She could barely speak, much less think.

'A way to kill two birds with one stone.'

'I don't understand.'

'I always told myself that if I ever saw you again, I'd cross to the other side of the street. Once was enough. I had moved beyond you, beyond your father, beyond that morning.'

Her heart twisted at the raw emotion in his words. 'Then why—'

'I was wrong.'

The admission seemed dragged from him.

'I still want you.'

She gasped, his words landing hard in her chest. 'Graciano—'

He moved his hand lower, pressing a finger to her lips. She tried to remember, to remember sense and logic and the fact they were parents to a daughter, that their situation was complicated, but in that moment, everything felt simple. A strong chemical urge was pushing her forward; to hell with their past.

'And you were there, offering yourself to the highest bidder. How could I not act on that opportunity?'

She swallowed, eyes huge when they met his. 'It's not... I'm not—'

'You're here to plan an event,' he said, moving his mouth to the pulse point at the base of her throat and pressing his lips there. 'But I have you here, in my home, for five nights, and I intend to make the most of them.'

CHAPTER THREE

'WHAT EXACTLY DOES that mean?'

Great question. Graciano had gone back and forth on this plan since it rammed itself into his damned head at the charity auction. Seducing Alicia for revenge appealed to him on so many levels, but it also disgusted him. It infuriated him that she still had any kind of power over him, even as he recognised he wanted to exert his own power right back over her.

To prove he was different to the lovesick eighteen-year-old she'd used and discarded. To show her that he'd grown into the kind of man she'd never thought he could be.

To make her want him as though he were her universe.

To walk away, as he had then, only this time memories of Alicia wouldn't torment his sleep, wouldn't make him want to weaken and return to her side because he'd be leaving her by *choice*.

This was his chance to show how far he'd come, how strong he now was. How completely in control. Revenge wasn't a particularly worthy emotion, but there was no other way to describe how Graciano felt, nor what he wanted. Was it petty, after ten years, to seek vengeance on a woman who'd moved on with her life, as he had his?

Something twisted in his gut, something dark and angry, something that made him face the truth of his character, something he hadn't known about himself. Yes, he would go to these lengths. Yes, he wanted revenge just this badly. Yes, he wanted to destroy her the way she'd destroyed him.

Because she had.

When her father had stood over Graciano and accused him of raping Alicia, Graciano had felt as though he'd been stabbed. He'd looked to her to speak some sense, to set her father straight, and she had only cowered, pinning herself to her father's side, the beautiful woman he'd made love to hours earlier someone he no longer recognised. She was a coward. She was a traitor. She had let Edward berate Graciano, calling him the worst names in the world, and she'd said nothing. Done nothing. When Edward had thrown Graciano off the property, telling him he'd call the police if he ever saw the eighteen-year-old again, she still hadn't said anything.

She'd chosen peace and her 'nice' life over truth, passion and Graciano, and he'd never forgotten that betrayal, nor forgiven her for it.

He hadn't thought of her consciously these past ten years, but the speed with which he'd sought his revenge made him wonder if he hadn't always wanted this, if he hadn't been looking for an opportunity to right the wrongs of the past.

It was petty, it was cruel, it was almost certainly something he'd regret, but Graciano was, as always, following his instincts. Heaven help him—levelling the score had never been so tempting.

Ten years ago, he'd been slow. Gentle. Cautious. He'd thought her fragile, and had been so wary of breaking her. They were both older and wiser now. He knew better.

'Graciano? What do you mean?' she repeated, with urgency, but her body remained where it was, close to him, so close he could breathe her in—so close he would have been in danger of losing himself, if such a thing were possible. Her sharp intake of breath and rapid exhalation brushed against his cheek. 'Graciano…'

There was so much he wanted to know and understand about this woman, so much he needed to comprehend in order to have closure. 'Why did you call me after I'd left?'

Her eyes fluttered closed, and he leaned in. One shift from either of them and their lips would brush. Her eyes opened and she started, but didn't move away from him. Her hand lifted, fingers pressed to his chest, and sensations rushed through Graciano. It was a worrying tilt away from control. He had to manage his needs, to master his wants. He wouldn't lose himself to her again.

'Why do you think?' Her eyes were pleading with his. 'I was mortified. I couldn't believe the things he'd said to you.' To his surprise, tears filmed her eyes. 'I couldn't believe I'd *let* him speak to you that way. But you have to understand—'

Sympathy was a danger he hadn't expected. He couldn't soften to her. 'I understand that you chose to let him think me a rapist rather than tell him the truth.'

'I did tell him the truth,' she said urgently, swallowing, her fingers curling in the fabric of his shirt. Surprise flashed through him, then swiftly, disbelief. He couldn't believe her—he didn't want to. 'I did. I just couldn't do it right then. I was too…shocked. Scared.' Her breath smelled like vanilla. He inhaled it, his arousal jerking against the fabric of his boxers.

Hell, he hadn't wanted a woman this badly in a long time. Possibly not for ten years.

He ignored her claims. He couldn't process them. His body was in sensory overload. 'And did you think I'd come back to you?'

'No,' she whispered, shuddering. 'I knew it wasn't possible. He'd have never allowed it.'

'And you always do what your father wants.'

She blinked down, away from him, shielding her thoughts from his gaze. 'I was sixteen.'

'Old enough to give yourself to me,' he reminded her firmly.

'And so what? Did you think I'd run away from home to live on the streets with you because we slept together? Is that what you wanted?'

It was like being doused with ice-cold water, reminding him of where her true priorities had lain. She'd chosen her 'nice' life of comfort rather than to stand by him. She'd wanted material security instead of the loyalty and love he'd thought they shared.

'After that morning, I didn't want a thing to do with you,' he corrected without any emotion in his voice. 'I don't believe in second chances.'

She pulled back a little, but kept her hand in his shirt. 'I just...needed to speak to you.'

'And yet, your actions were the making of me, *querida*. I left Seville, I grew up, I changed. I forgot all about you.'

Her eyes barely met his. 'Good for you.'

'Yet here we are, ten years later, and I can't help but wonder...'

'What do you wonder?' she asked, unable to keep the husky note from her voice.

'What it would feel like to kiss you,' he said simply, eyes skimming hers, seeing the awakening there, the desire, unmistakable. 'Not as we were then—teenagers—but here, now, two adults, with experience behind us...'

'Graciano...' His name was a plea. For sanity, or seduction?

'Do you wonder the same?'

Her lips parted, and it was Alicia who moved closer now, her eyes hooked to his, uncertainty and fear in their depths, and a strange, angry mix of emotions in his gut that he would be ashamed to analyse later.

'I can't,' she said, so close to him he felt the words rather than heard them.

'You don't want to?'

She shook her head. 'It's complicated.'

'Is it? Why?'

Her lips quirked downwards. 'Because you're you,' she responded softly.

'We are completely alone here,' he said gruffly. 'Neither of us has to be ourselves for the next week.'

Her eyes widened.

'Besides, a kiss is just a kiss.'

She made a throaty sound, her fingers in his shirt twisting, holding on to him as if for dear life. 'I don't know if that's true.'

He'd never wanted to kiss a woman more. Not even Alicia, not even back then. There was a force at his back, a steel-like drive pushing him to her, and yet he held his ground, determined to triumph over even his own desire.

'I will not kiss you unless you ask it of me.'

She bit down into her lip. 'I can't do that.' Her eyes showed confusion. 'I won't. Graciano, our past—'

'The past is irrelevant to this,' he interrupted angrily, even when he knew the past had defined him in every way that mattered.

'Graciano…' Now his name was unmistakably a plea, and she leaned in, surrendering to him, so he exulted in the victory as he crushed his lips to hers, claiming her with all the need, anger and resentment that had stitched their way into his soul a long time ago.

Alicia almost jumped with the electrical current that arced inside of her when their lips touched. This was not a gentle kiss. It was not a kiss of two people reconnecting after years apart. It was a kiss of total dominance and, yes, of anger. She felt it in the bruising way he commanded her, demanded of her, and yet she didn't—couldn't—mind. She was angry, too, angry in a way she'd never allowed herself to be because of how futile that anger was. But how could she not feel it now? The waste of it all. The devastation wrought by her father's behaviour, by Graciano's disappearance.

She'd had their child, and kept her a secret from him.

He'd said the past was irrelevant. He'd said they weren't themselves this week. And if that were true, then anger wouldn't matter, but they couldn't really step out of the past.

Anger was a natural way to feel, for both of them.

Her hand in his shirt moved to his shoulder and she was pulling him harshly down on top of her, fury swirling with hunger and need and fear, because Graciano had awakened something inside of Alicia she'd thought long dead.

A voice in her head screamed at her to stop this madness, to see sense, but she'd done the sensible and right thing for ten long years and Lord if she didn't want to give in to desire just once, now. To satiate a hunger that had overtaken her, not bit by bit, but rather as an avalanche, all at once.

'Please,' she groaned against his neck as he moved his mouth to the flesh beneath her ear, then dragged it lower, to the pulse point at the base of her throat. He flicked his tongue against her skin and she whimpered, squirming, because her body was alive with flames and only he had the power to douse them. But first, he stirred them, fanning them, making her too hot, too desperately hungry for him. He lifted up a litle, staring down at her with an expression she couldn't understand, and then his hands pulled at her shirt, popping the top two buttons to reveal the delicate lace of her bra.

She panted as his hand moved to cup the underside of one breast, as if appraising it, evaluating it. She lifted her pelvis, no longer in control of her body, totally overcome by needs that were beyond her ability to temper.

His fingers brushed her nipple and she cried out, the touch electric and intimate, and so unfamiliar. Not since Graciano had anyone done this to her.

Always, he'd had this power over her.

Always, she'd been his.

But he'd never been hers. Not really.

Where she had loved him completely, and carried that love inside her, along with their child, he'd moved on as soon as he'd left Seville. The broken pieces of her life had been hard to order. How she'd needed him in that first year. How she'd pined for him.

Her grief flooded her, reminding her of the catastrophic after-effects of what had happened between them, and it was enough to kill her libido, to douse the fever pitch of need he'd stirred so ruthlessly.

'Stop.' She pressed a hand to his chest now,

her breathing uneven, panic making her skin pale and clammy. 'We have to stop this.'

Oh, God. What had she been thinking? She couldn't be kissing this man! She shouldn't even have agreed to come here. Everything was far too complicated. They shared a daughter, a daughter he knew nothing about. She'd kept Annie from him and at first that had made sense. But now? What justification did she have for lying to him about their daughter? How could she explain it?

It was so complicated and tangled, and terrifying, because Annie was *her* daughter. Graciano had given up his claim on her a long time ago. At least, that's what Alicia had been telling herself. But could a parent ever really give up on their own child, without being informed of the child's existence?

Panic set in, pummelling her lungs so the air left them completely and she couldn't reinflate them no matter how hard she tried. Her eyes filled with stars and her skin drained of all colour.

She wasn't conscious of much, except for Graciano's steady, confident hands lifting her into a seated position, then bringing her head forward, dropping it lower, his hand on her back rubbing rhythmically, his voice, Spanish words, low and soft, musical, reminding her of the way he'd spoken to her in Spanish back then, teaching her phrases, helping her learn his dialect.

Tears filled her eyes, but at least she could breathe again.

He evidently felt the steadiness return because he pushed to standing and moved away from her, staring out of the window for several long seconds, which she used to pull her shirt back together as best she could when the buttons were missing.

'That was a mistake,' she whispered, quivering fingers lifting to her lips and pressing against them. She closed her eyes and saw Annie's face and felt as though she'd been felled at the knees. She was a mother first. Her personal wishes were a lot less important than what she owed to Annie.

He turned to face her slowly, hands on hips, expression impossible to read—only there was darkness in the set of his features, a danger that made her tremble.

Whatever love there'd been between them, even if it was just from her, had turned to something else. Something dark and angry. Hate.

'You don't want me to kiss you again?'

Her eyes lowered. What she wanted? It was better not to explore that. 'It can't happen again,' she repeated instead.

'There is unfinished business between us, with only one way to resolve it.'

Promise hummed between them, a fierce, undeniable pull into temptation and desire. She bit down on her lip to stop herself from agreeing with him verbally, but in her heart, she knew he was right.

All the reasons she had to keep him at bay paled in comparison to the fact that she wanted him, desperately—that she needed him with all of herself. Maybe here, on this little island, she truly was in an oasis, away from Annie and her duties to their daughter, away from the life she'd carefully built for herself. Maybe, just maybe, she could be reckless and no harm would come from that, this time. Or *maybe*, she should run like hell rather than give into temptation for the second time in her life.

Alicia had been strong this past decade: strong when she'd stood up to her father; strong when he'd exiled her from Spain and stranded her in England with a grandmother she hardly knew; strong when she'd become a single mother at sixteen; strong as she'd raised Annie single-handedly…and she needed to be strong now.

'You're wrong, Graciano.' She spoke quietly, but with a hint of steel. 'There is nothing unfinished between us. You finished it, when you disappeared into thin air—when you refused to return my calls, when you ceased to exist in my life.' She stood, knees shaking a little. 'I know that my father treated you like dirt—worse than dirt—but you left without a backwards glance. You left without—'

'Without what, *querida*?' The term of endearment caused her to flinch. 'Your father was not the only one who treated me like dirt. True, he spoke the words, but you echoed them with your silence.' His eyes narrowed. 'What was I supposed to do? Stay and be arrested for a crime I never committed? For a crime so heinous—' He let the words hang there, his pride obviously wounded. His nostrils flared and he crossed his arms over his broad chest, staring down at her with darkly intense emotions swirling in his eyes.

Alicia couldn't bring herself to respond to that. The idea of Graciano being charged with rape after what they'd shared turned her blood to ice. But she couldn't be derailed from the point she needed to hammer home. 'All those years ago, that was the time to explore our unfinished business. Not now.' She pulled herself up to her full height. 'Now if you'll excuse me, I have work to do, and the sooner I finish, and can get off this island, the better.'

CHAPTER FOUR

ALICIA STARED AT her laptop without seeing any of the information on the screen. She'd spent the afternoon researching—previous events Graciano had hosted, the companies he'd bought, the events his enormous corporation had thrown, anything that would give her an insight into what he wanted without actually having to talk to him about it.

Which was childish and stupid.

Despite what had happened between them, she'd come here to do a job, and she wasn't about to ignore her obligations on that front.

Her ankle was still tender, but far better than it had been, courtesy of the painkillers he'd provided her with hours earlier before helping her to a guest room where she'd changed into a shirt with all the buttons in place.

But as she looked out at the glistening sea beyond her window, she couldn't help but regret that she'd only packed business clothes.

It had been an act of defiance at the time, a demarcation of her purpose at Graciano's. A statement of intent.

She'd planned to wear her suits and heels,

to provide a starkly visible reminder to both of them, at all times, that she was there to work.

Had she anticipated, even then, that desire would overcome them? Probably, but she'd expected to make it through at least one hour without wanting to rip his clothes off.

She looked across at her bed ruefully, to the discarded shirt there, and grimaced, then turned her attention back to the screen.

It was hard work—not because it was difficult to pull together a profile on what Graciano's events were like. She had a clear idea of that. But because events hosted by Graciano featured a lot of Graciano, and by necessity, she'd spent most of the afternoon staring at photographs of him dressed in custom tuxedos surrounded by stunning guests, many of whom were glamorous women looking at Graciano as though…as though they wanted everything Alicia did.

She moaned, dropping her head into her hands, mortified and made alive in equal measure by memories of what they'd done that afternoon. Her heart raced faster with adrenaline as she contemplated how wonderful it had felt to be kissed by him.

Except he wasn't just a handsome man with whom she shared a past. The matter of Annie was a sharp knife pressing into her side, something she was struggling to make sense of.

Contacting Graciano once he was worth all the money in the world, just about, hadn't been easy. There was a wall around him. His phone number was unattainable, his location unknown, security tight. Even when she'd woken in the middle of the night, body coated in the perspiration of the panicked, and she'd realised she couldn't keep Annie a secret from her father, she'd had no idea *how* to tell him.

Until he'd turned up at the charity auction, he'd been as out of reach to Alicia as any other billionaire or celebrity.

But they were here together now. The conversation could be had. And then what?

She groaned softly, closed the laptop and jerked to standing, a frown on her face that was a copy of the ache in her heart.

If Graciano had intentionally planned to seduce Alicia with his lifestyle, he couldn't have chosen a better location. She'd expected to grab a piece of fruit for dinner, but when she walked slowly out of her room on an ankle that was feeling much better and went in search of the kitchen, she found a table for two had been set in the middle of the courtyard. She stopped walking, staring first at it—the white cloth, the wine bottle, the candles and crystal glasses—and then looked around, taking in the broader aspect automatically. It was her first opportunity to regard the courtyard properly, and now she saw details she couldn't possibly have appreciated from the air.

A large staircase led up one side of the courtyard to a balcony that wrapped around the internal walls, and it was these walls that vines tumbled over, cascading like floral waterfalls towards the ground, creating a feast for the eyes and a heavenly fragrance. Bees hummed around the blooms and birds twittered overhead. Terracotta pots marked the base of each pillar, and fruit trees, perfectly topiarised and large, broke up the effect of the wall. The sky overhead was turning to dusky colours, and lights had come on around the walls, creating a warmth and ambience that made Alicia feel she was in a five-star resort—but even better, because it wasn't so pristine and manicured.

There was whimsy and charm here, and so much history. She looked around once more, right as Graciano emerged into the courtyard, head bent as though deep in thought, so she had a moment to study him, and pull herself together, before he saw her.

He wore beige shorts and a loose white linen shirt, the quintessential image of relaxed charm—only Graciano, she suspected, never truly relaxed. It wasn't in his nature. Even as an eighteen-year-old, there'd been a drive about

him. It was why his father had employed Graciano at the homestead, rather than just the mission home.

'That boy never stops,' Edward had mar-
velled, again and again. 'Just look at him go.'

And Alicia *had* looked. She'd looked until
her tummy had been in knots and she'd wanted
things that made no sense to her. Her mouth went
dry as memories flooded her, memories that left
her flushed with warm, moist heat between her
legs as Graciano approached, his uniquely masculine fragrance reaching her nostrils and sending her pulse tripping.

'Hungry?'

'Yes,' she said truthfully.

His eyes met hers and something sparked in
her bloodstream. She swallowed hard, looking
away.

'Please, have a seat.' Such civility, but she
felt the hum between them, the intensity of his
words. As she moved to a seat, he pulled it back
for her. She sat, and his hands glanced her shoulders briefly—the softest caress, but enough to
lift her flesh with goosebumps.

'Thank you,' she murmured, as he came to
sit opposite her.

She opened her mouth to say something, but
a moment later, footsteps heralded the arrival of

a slender woman with greying hair and a crinkled face.

'Isabella.' Graciano dipped his head in acknowledgement. The older woman's grin was one of easy affection.

'It is nice to see you back, sir.'

'It's nice to be back. Isabella, this is a colleague of mine. Miss Griffiths.'

Alicia's skin prickled for a different reason now: dislike. She heard it in the way he rumbled the syllables of her surname—her father's surname—and felt all his enmity barrelling towards her.

'Alicia,' she responded with a taut smile of her own.

'Alicia,' Isabella repeated. 'It is a pleasure to welcome you here. Would you like some wine to start?'

Terrible idea. Wine would only loosen her already non-existent inhibitions. 'I—' But at the same time, her nerves were frayed beyond bearing. One glass might help her get through the night without dissolving into a jumble of anxiety at Graciano's feet. 'Yes, wine would be lovely, thank you.'

'A bottle of the Rioja,' he said, smiling, and her heart tripped over itself, so pleased—so surprised—to see that on his features.

Isabella nodded and disappeared through a pair of timber doors.

'I thought you said we were completely alone.'

His eyes zeroed in on hers, and she shivered as their connection sparked inside her bloodstream, his smile shifting into an appraising expression. 'Disappointed?'

She couldn't admit that, even to herself. 'Relieved, in fact.'

The quirk of his lips showed he didn't believe her. 'There is a skeleton crew on the island. Isabella is my housekeeper.'

'Does she live here?' Alicia gestured to the mansion that surrounded them.

'You might have noticed cabins across the island as you flew over?'

'I presumed they were for guests.'

'Some are. Some are for my permanent staff.'

'How many are there?'

'Eighteen cabins.'

'I meant staff.'

'Four. Isabella, my chef Juanita, a gardener, Rodrigo, and Luis, who runs security.'

The same security who'd made it impossible to contact him all those years ago, when she'd wanted to tell him about the daughter they shared.

Isabella returned at that moment, and beside her stood a young woman, perhaps nineteen or twenty. She blushed when she looked at Graciano, and Alicia pitied her. She knew the power of the man opposite her. What woman would be able to resist his charms?

Alicia looked away as Isabella poured two glasses of wine and the young girl placed a platter of tapas before them—chorizo, breads, olives, cheese, fruit and little tartlets with anchovies and garlic.

When they were alone, she couldn't resist asking, 'Your chef?'

'One of Isabella's projects,' he said with an air of affection that ripped Alicia's own heart out. For a moment, she caught a glimpse of the boy Graciano had been, the boy who'd had all the time in the world for her—who, despite his awful upbringing, had always smiled for her.

The sense of loss was dazzling.

That boy no longer existed for Alicia, but he did for others.

'Projects?' she queried, reaching for her wine and taking a gulp, so glad for the relief she didn't notice the delicious flavour until her second sip.

'She recruits people from the streets,' he said, eyes focused straight ahead. He was looking at Alicia without really seeing her. 'She cares only that they work hard and don't do drugs—her two rules.'

Alicia's heart shifted in her chest. 'Does she know about your time living rough?'

'It's something she and I have in common.'

Alicia leaned forward a little. 'Isabella, too?'

'She was one of the first I hired.'

'All your staff come from that background?'

'What's the point of employing people if not to give them a second chance? Here, they have a roof over their heads, a good job. Like Isabella, I have very few rules.'

She sipped her wine again. 'What are your rules?'

'Honesty and loyalty.'

Alicia flicked her gaze down to the table. From Graciano's perspective, Alicia had failed him on that front.

'And qualifications?'

'In my opinion, people can become qualified in anything if they're motivated enough, and nothing motivates like having lived on the streets.'

'When you left Seville—'

'When your father threw me out?'

Parched throat, she nodded. 'I worried about you.'

His eyes narrowed.

'I hated the thought of you going back to the streets. Some of the things you'd told me—the things you'd done, the things that happened to you… I couldn't sleep for fear of how you were living.'

Silence crackled between them, broken occasionally by the tweeting of an evening bird drifting overhead.

'Your worry was redundant. As you can see, I was fine.'

'But how?' she asked, urgently, leaning forward, then reaching for her wine and forcing herself to relax. 'How did you do all this?'

'Do you suspect a crime? That I somehow stole my fortune, Alicia?'

Her pulse kicked up a gear at the sound of her name in his mouth.

'Of course not.'

'Or that I became a gigolo to some wealthy woman and swindled her of her fortune?'

'That hadn't even occurred to me,' she muttered. 'Though if it had, you'd have only yourself to blame. Do you remember what you said to me the second time I called? The last time we spoke?'

His face gave nothing away; his features remained set in an iron-like mask.

'You told me you'd found someone else to have sex with. That's how you described it. I sacrificed everything for you and you—'

'What did you sacrifice for me?' he demanded. 'Did you think my life was a bed of roses after I told my father the truth?' she demanded fiercely. 'How do you think he reacted? What do you think he did?'

It was obvious that Graciano hadn't contemplated that. 'I had no idea that you would tell him the truth after I'd left. You certainly showed no intention of it that morning.'

'Of course I did,' she spat. 'That morning, I was in shock. I was terrified, and ashamed—a lifetime's conditioning is hard to shake. My father's messages of purity and innocence were pressed deep into my soul. But I did tell him later, and my world fell apart. I called you because I needed you, Graciano. I needed you.' It was impossible to keep her bitter resentment from her voice. 'And you turned what we were, what we'd been, into something so sordid, into an irrelevancy. You'd replaced me. That was that.'

A muscle jerked in his jaw; otherwise, he didn't react.

'Is that really how you felt?'

He took a sip of his own wine—his first. 'What do you want from me?' he asked after a moment, replacing the glass with deliberate care. 'After all this time, do you want me to say I lied? That I hadn't moved on? That I missed you? That I needed you, too?'

'Only if it's true.'

He stared at her long and hard and she held her breath, but a moment later, the young woman reappeared, carrying more food—steaks and potatoes and a salad.

When they were alone again, the fight had left Alicia. She felt stunned and numb, too devastated by their conversation to pick it up again.

Evidently, Graciano had the same lack of appetite for continuing that train of thought.

'There are two options for the party,' he said, taking a pair of tongs and using them to move food onto her plate first—far more than she could possibly eat, but she sat silently as he heaped steak and potatoes and beans and rocket, then olives and flans in front of her. She finished her wine, then replaced the empty glass.

'This courtyard makes sense. It's close to the kitchens, and the ground is steady, which is saying something, as much of this side of the island is mountainous.'

She wondered at the ease with which he'd pivoted to business; then again, none of this really mattered to Graciano. He'd moved on, as he'd been at pains to point out.

'However, there is a spot down near the beach, also nice and flat, and the drama of the cliffs and the ocean would make a spectacular backdrop as the sun goes down.'

Alicia tried to kick her brain into gear, but she

was spinning wildly out of control so one plus one wouldn't equal two, no matter how hard she tried to make it.

'I'll need some more information on the kind of party,' she said eventually, the words coming out far flatter than she'd realised.

'Now is your chance. Ask whatever you want.'

The problem was that what she wanted to know had nothing to do with the party. She toyed with her napkin in her lap as Graciano refilled her glass. 'You said around one hundred people?'

'Yes. Intimate. The directors of the company I'm buying, the directors of my own company. Some valued staff.'

'Friends?' she prompted, curious about the life he was leading.

His brow lifted. He knew what she was asking.

'Do you mean girlfriends of mine, specifically, Alicia?'

Her cheeks flamed, caught out before she'd even realised what she was asking. 'Well, you do date.'

'That's one way to describe it.'

Heat infused her cheeks. 'Really? It's always just about sex for you?'

'It's rarely about more,' he said with a lift of his shoulders.

She pounced on that, wondering what kind of glutton for punishment she was. 'But sometimes it is?'

'Does it make any difference to your plans if I have a lover here with me or not?'

A lover. So sensual. So intimate. So difficult to contemplate. She dug her fingernails into her palms and stared straight ahead.

'A party is a party, no?'

'Yes,' she said, her voice husky. She took a gulp of wine to massage her vocal cords back into submission.

'So this is personal interest alone?'

She dropped her gaze to the mountain of food in front of her and lifted her fork, spearing an olive. 'Yes.' There was no point in lying. As she'd explained, her curiosity was not only natural, it was reciprocal.

'I'm not seeing any one particular woman at the moment.'

'Are you seeing more than one woman?'

'I am always "dating".'

'Like the redhead from the charity ball? I wonder what she would think of you bringing me here like this?'

'She wouldn't care. Caroline is under no illusions about my monogamy.'

The jealousy was unmistakable. It almost sheared her in two. She lifted her eyes to him, shocked by the visceral reaction—angry with it, too. It had been ten damned years. Of course he'd been with many, many other women since her. She knew that to be fact, so why did this hurt so much?

Because they were face to face, and time was no longer a linear constant but a vortex into which she could be sucked backwards. Sitting across from Graciano, they could be a decade younger, two hearts beating in unison, their futures unmapped, hope still a credible notion.

'Good for you,' she muttered to fill the silence and kill the hopeful sentiment.

His laugh was low and soft. It drifted across the table towards her, wrapping around her like a vice, as beneath the table, his leg kicked forward, his ankle brushing hers so she was trapped and stunned, stuck like a bug in a spider's web.

'Careful, Alicia. You sound jealous.'

'I'm not,' she spat. 'Believe me.'

He lifted a brow, that same mocking smile tilting his lips.

She drove her fork into a piece of meat with anger. 'Why would I be jealous?' she demanded, the question one she was trying to answer herself. 'What happened between us was over years ago. We've both moved on.'

'Yes,' he agreed easily, quickly, but his eyes narrowed slightly and he watched her intently, so her throat was parched. 'And yet, when I kissed you—'

'I already told you, that was a mistake. It won't happen again.' Something clutched in her chest, but she had to be strong. There was too much at stake to be drawn into conversations about their past, their chemistry. 'Just…drop it, Graciano. I'm here to work.' She blurted the reminder into the air between them, as if she could verbally raise a shield. She really just hoped it would hold out for the week.

CHAPTER FIVE

ALICIA TOLD HERSELF she was delighted that she didn't see Graciano the next morning. She dressed in a suit, for lack of other options, and worked for several hours in her bedroom before hunger drove her out in search of some fruit or something light to eat. Isabella was dusting in the lounge room and intercepted Alicia, all too willing to help her with a far more substantial breakfast than Alicia had envisaged. Nonetheless, it was nice to be fussed over, and the savoury omelette, fresh-baked bread and butter, and coffee was a delicious way to start the day.

As she cooked, Isabella chatted, and every third word was 'Graciano'. Graciano is so kind, so thoughtful, Graciano works too hard, Graciano is very generous, so Alicia found herself nodding and barely listening until, eventually, she said, 'And where is Graciano today?'

Isabella had smiled apologetically, perhaps mistaking Alicia's question for a desire to see the man, rather than avoid him. 'He has flown to Barcelona, for work. I told you, he's always working.' She shook her head, but smiled as she placed another coffee in front of Alicia.

Alicia doubted he was *always* working. After

all, he'd been at pains to point out how active his love life was.

For Alicia, Graciano's absence meant opportunity. It also meant she could breathe freely. 'Do you think he'd mind if I had a look around?' She gestured to her laptop. 'It's for *my* work.'

'He would not have brought you here if he did not trust you. Just let me know if you need my help with anything.'

Alicia didn't express her scepticism of that to the housekeeper. 'Thank you.'

'What time would you like to eat lunch?'

'Lunch? I don't think I'll need it after that delicious breakfast.'

'You must eat! This is Spain—the food is too good to refuse. I have some marinated octopus and rice. I'll put together something light. Say one o'clock?'

Alicia could see it was pointless to argue so she nodded.

'In the courtyard.' Isabella nodded with satisfaction, pleased with having won Alicia over.

That gave Alicia a few hours in which to properly tour the house and surrounds, and she didn't intend to waste a moment of it. Pausing only to fill up her water bottle, she started with the house, peering into rooms with open doors, avoiding those that were closed or locked, not wanting to stumble upon Graciano's bedroom or anything else too personal.

The house itself was quite fascinating, obviously old, but beautifully preserved, as though someone had spent a fortune renovating it at some point—as evidenced by the new wiring and air conditioning—while preserving the original features. Parquetry floors, mosaic tiles, elaborate murals and wall carvings… It was ornate and beautiful.

It was also the last place she could ever have imagined Graciano.

But then, as she walked, she remembered snatches of conversations—when he'd admired the sconces of her father's home, or explained the history of the building to her from the arches to the windows.

Where had she imagined he might live?

Had she thought he would always be homeless and penniless?

No. She simply hadn't thought that far ahead. She had imagined, in some strange way, that they would be always together, and at sixteen, hadn't been able to foresee a life distinct from her father.

Bitterness flooded her mouth and she wilfully pushed those thoughts from her mind.

The upper story of the mansion could easily be repurposed. A large dining hall could be used to house a band. With the doors open, four musicians could be on the balcony itself, and the rest would add depth to the songs. The magnificent staircase would have flowers wound around the railings, and party lights could be strung over the whole courtyard to create the feeling of a carnival.

Tables and chairs would be in the centre, with floaty white cloths and flower arrangements to play up the colours of the vines. It would easily accommodate the number of tables required, she thought, imagining round tables at first before changing her mind and envisaging two lengths, a classic banquet setting, to capture the drama of the perfectly square courtyard.

Ideas came to her as she walked, so when Isabella appeared in the courtyard at one, she was startled out of her reverie.

'Lunch time already? My goodness, that went fast.'

'Graciano has asked you to join him on the terrace.'

'Graciano?' She went from relaxed to anxious in the flash of an eye. 'I thought he was in Barcelona?'

Isabella shrugged, nonplussed. 'His meetings must have finished early, eh? Do you know the way?'

She was tempted to ignore his request, but she

was a professional and this was, first and foremost, a job. She was being paid to be here—or the charity was—and her personal code of ethics refused to allow her to give anything less than her best.

'No.' She flattened her lips. 'Would you mind showing me?'

Graciano seemed to be deep in thought when she walked through a set of wrought iron gates framed with bougainvillea and onto a delightful terrace that overlooked the ocean. The view was so breathtaking she had to pause a moment to appreciate it, to inhale the fragrance of sea salt and tropical flowers, before turning back to him and then, immediately, wishing she hadn't. He wore another suit, navy blue this time, but he'd discarded the jacket and tie over the back of a chair and undone the shirt at his throat so her eyes immediately dropped to the thick column there and the sprinkling of hair that was revealed. Her mouth went dry and her legs felt hollow.

Graciano stood, and the action broke the effect of her concentration. She wrenched her gaze away, drawing in a breath, trying to calm her scattered nerves.

'I've been exploring the house,' she blurted out, willing him not to make one of his sarcastic remarks about the way she was staring at him like a lovesick teenager.

'Isabella mentioned.'

'Is she spying on me?' Alicia asked with surprise, moving to the seat opposite Graciano but pausing before easing herself into it.

'Not at all. She likes to talk. Perhaps you noticed? She mentioned you've been poking around in all the rooms.'

'Not all of them,' Alicia was quick to refute. 'I've been careful not to open any doors.'

'There is nothing you cannot see,' he dismissed with a shrug.

'I didn't want to invade your privacy.'

'By stepping into my bedroom? I'll live.'

But she might not have. She was already finding it hard to breathe. The thought of seeing his private space, of being surrounded by its masculinity, made her head spin. When he'd stayed with them all those years ago, he'd slept in a dormitory her father had repurposed for runaways in need of safe haven—at least, that's what her father had said. Now, she saw it more as exploitative. Free labour. There had frequently been two or three hand-picked teens staying with them at any one time. Graciano hadn't had a bedroom of his own. Nor had he had any possessions, so Alicia hadn't ever seen his room, nor could she imagine what it would be like. But she was better not knowing.

'How long have you lived here?' she asked after a moment.

'I don't live here.' Isabella appeared with an elaborate tray—octopus, rice salad, fruit, cheese and bread. When they were alone again, he continued. 'I split my time between the island, Barcelona and London.'

Her heart went into overdrive far too fast for her to cope with. She pretended interest with the glass of mineral water he was pouring, her eyes tracing the bubbles, all the while her pulse frantically moving into dangerous territory. 'London?' she murmured, hoping for nonchalance but aware the word came out strained.

'I have an office there.'

She swallowed, but her throat was thick, nerves all bunched together.

'Do you go often?'

'For about a week every month. Why?'

She bit down on her lip, toying with her fingers in her lap. She lived in a sleepy little part of zone three, in a hook on the river. It wasn't as though they were likely to run into each other. But the idea of Graciano having been within a tube ride of Alicia—and Annie—all these years, and Alicia having not known, made her head spin, and her heart ache. It was all so impossible.

'I'm just trying to get a picture of your life now.'

'Does it help you plan the event?'

'It doesn't hurt,' she said honestly, then sighed, deciding honesty was the best policy—at least with this. 'But more so, I'm just curious. You've come so far. I'm interested in how you live. In how you did it.'

'I worked hard.'

'But doing what?' she pushed. 'Within six months of leaving Seville, you were a high-end realtor. That's not something you had experience with.'

'Real estate is about people, and I had a lot of experience with them.'

It was casually said, but she felt the sting in the words. She thought of the experience her father—and Alicia—had given him, and fought an urge to wince.

He took a drink of water. 'I found it easy,' he said after a moment. 'I was good at understanding what people wanted, how to give it to them. I'd spent years on the streets—I had an innate understanding of property, values, the quality of one neighbourhood versus another, and I was strongly motivated to succeed. I didn't sleep for at least three months. I chased down every lead, sold every house, met every vendor, drove buyers from the airport all around Madrid. By the end of the first year, I was earning more than a million euros in commissions.'

Her lips parted on a rush. 'You must have been so...thrilled.'

'Thrilled? No, Alicia.' She shivered as he caressed her name. 'I was hungry. I wanted *more*. You couldn't possibly understand. You've never felt that way—to worry about when you will eat again, where you will sleep. To me, it wasn't possible to *ever* earn enough. It's still not.'

She shook her head sadly. 'But you're worth a fortune.'

'Yes.'

'And this place?'

She gestured around them.

His smile set her blood on fire. It was so intimate, so natural. So genuine. It made her crave the connection they had once shared.

'I wanted it the minute I saw it.'

She nodded slowly. 'It's beautiful.'

'Yes.' He leaned back in his chair, looking around them. 'The history is unique.'

'What is the history?'

'Ferdinand the seventh built it for his mistress.'

She frowned. 'Is he the guy with a penchant for marrying his nieces?'

Graciano grinned and bubbles formed in her blood as she was plunged back into the past, when he'd smiled at her so readily. 'This was not built for a niece, but for a woman he apparently loved very deeply. Perhaps you saw the turret while you were exploring this morning?'

She shook her head. 'No, I didn't. Where is it?'

'I'll show you later. It's not important. But it was built as a lookout, so that she could watch for his arrival. He came by boat, of course. He was jealous and guarded her fiercely—he was the only visitor she ever had.'

'That's...' She searched for the right word. 'Kind of sad.'

He lifted a brow, silently prompting her to continue.

'As time went on, he visited less and less, but she watched for him always.'

'What happened to her?'

'She went mad.'

'Mad?'

'Completely crazy, yes.'

'How awful.'

'Yes.' He lifted his shoulders. 'But interesting.'

She looked around, seeing the place through new eyes now. 'It's very grand, for one person.'

'There was an army of staff as well.'

'Naturally,' Alicia agreed with a hint of a smile. 'Perhaps she found happiness with one of them. A secret affair that history forgot, by virtue of how well they guarded their transgression.'

'You'd prefer to think she fell out of love than stayed loyal?'

'To the point of insanity? While he went about his business, marrying woman after woman? Yes, I'd infinitely prefer to think she found some level of happiness independent of him.'

'Is the idea of loyalty in the face of adversity so hard to imagine?'

'This isn't about loyalty,' she said after a beat. 'He hid her away here for his pleasure, but only when he saw fit to visit. Meanwhile, she lost her youth, her life and finally her mind. What of his loyalty? His obligations?'

'She had a choice in the matter, I presume.'

'That's presuming a lot,' she muttered, well aware that agency was a matter of perspective.

'You think he kept her against her will?'

'A gilded cage is still a cage.'

'It's a leap to suggest she wanted to leave but couldn't.'

'Loneliness literally drove her mad. I don't think it's that great a leap.'

'And what would you have done?'

She didn't hesitate. 'I'd have swum to shore.'

'Even if you loved him?'

'That's not love.'

'How can you be so sure?'

'You disagree?'

'I asked first.'

She pulled a face. 'Love isn't selfish,' she said finally, and with authority. 'What he did was. Ergo, it wasn't love.'

'So black and white,' he murmured. 'You don't make any allowance for nuance?'

'You make way too many allowances,' she corrected carefully. 'You're predisposed to iden-tify with him. Rich, powerful man.'

'Capturing a woman for the purpose of sex? Really, Alicia?'

'Well, I mean…' Heat flushed her cheeks. 'If I hadn't stopped us yesterday…' She couldn't complete the sentence.

'Then let me be clear. You are free to leave at any point, and I will not even make you swim to shore. My helicopter is at your disposal.'

She tilted her face away, breathing forced and wretched as she tried to get to grips with how their conversation had reached this point. When-ever she tried to focus on the job she'd come to do, they got carried away and she lost command of things.

Sucking in a deep breath, she turned back to him resolutely. 'I'm not a quitter, Graciano.' The words were husky. 'I'll stay until I've finished organising your event.'

'Four more nights,' he said, and she shivered, because there was a challenge in his statement, and oh, so much promise.

Graciano read the message carefully, once more.

Hi, handsome. I'm in Barcelona for the night. Join me?

With a devil emoji, then a flame emoji.

Anastasia was one of the world's most renowned lingerie models, and he'd always enjoyed their time together. She was intelligent, interesting, beautiful and, most importantly of all, completely casual. She hated the idea of commitment, so catching up with her was always a pleasure.

His finger hovered over the screen and he paused, uncharacteristically indecisive. His office was on the top floor of the home and had windows on both sides. From one, he could see the ocean, sparkling all the way to mainland Spain. From the other, he looked down on the courtyard and across it, towards the turret.

Quite by chance, he moved to the back windows, with the vantage point of the internal walls, right as Alicia moved across the courtyard, a notepad in her hands. She was writing furiously, looking around, squinting, eyes chasing the windows, so he moved back a little. But there was no need to hide. She was looking at the windows without really seeing. Her mind was busy imagining, planning, preparing for the event he'd created out of thin air, simply to justify bringing her here. He watched, fascinated by this side of her.

More fascinated by her than he wanted to be—certainly more than he'd anticipated he'd feel. This week was supposed to be about showing her how different he was to the young, impressionable eighteen-year-old she'd used and discarded. It was supposed to be about making her want him, to enjoy the chemistry they shared and then walk away on *his* terms.

But since she'd arrived on the island, they'd sparred and sparked. Time spent with her was a unique agony of desire and desperation, anger and anticipation. For two days, she'd been right here, within arm's reach, and yet he knew nothing more about her than he had a week ago.

And suddenly, that wasn't good enough.

They had a finite amount of time together—there was nothing on earth that would convince him to pursue her beyond this week—and it was slipping through his fingers.

He wanted to bed her, undoubtedly. But he also wanted to understand her. To answer questions that were lingering in his mind. To put the whole matter to rest, once and for all.

She lifted a hand, rubbing the back of her neck, then closing her eyes and stretching as if in pain. He was frozen to the spot, unable to tear his eyes from her. Her fingers moved delicately lower, needling the tops of her shoulder so his own fingers began to tingle with a desire to replace hers.

Abruptly, she dropped her hands to her sides. Her phone was ringing.

He watched her scan the screen and smile, then lift it to her ear. The look on her face made his gut fall to his feet with the force of a rock boulder. Happiness. Pleasure. Contentment.

Whoever she was talking to made her look so damned joyous. He'd never known that feeling. Or not for ten years, at least.

'You brought me coffee?' She stared at the outstretched mug with scepticism, feelings she couldn't decipher fluttering in her chest. 'Why?'

'A peace offering,' he said, with a lift of his shoulders. Her eyes dropped to the impressive breadth there, to the strength of his frame, and her mouth went dry, so she reached for the coffee and took a quick, grateful sip. It wasn't hot enough to burn her mouth, thankfully.

'You look surprised.'

'You aren't someone to make peace.'

He laughed, the sound melodious and warm and, oh, so dangerous. 'How do you know, Alicia?' Her name on his lips rolled over her, so she pulled her lips to the side, fighting a smile of her own.

'Because you're stubborn and—'

'And what?'

'—angry,' she said quietly, honestly, peeping at him from beneath her lashes. 'Like you used to be before—'

Their eyes met and held. She didn't need to finish the sentence. He'd been angry, with a huge chip on his shoulder, when he'd arrived at the mission, but over the summer, as they'd got to know one another, he'd changed, morphing into a different man altogether.

'I am not angry, in fact,' he said with a lift of his shoulders. 'At least, not often.'

'Not with anyone but me?' She couldn't resist asking.

His smile almost felled her at the knees. 'You are more direct than you used to be.'

'I've had to be.'

'Why?' He was studying her, his body a study in nonchalance, but she knew him better than that.

She hesitated, sipping her coffee again, the feeling of the afternoon sun warming her back.

The ocean air, salty and mysterious, called to her, and again, she rued her decision to only bring corporate clothing.

'I suppose we all become more confident over time. I was just a girl back then.'

'*Si,*' he agreed, and her heart stammered because understanding that brought them one step closer to forgiveness; until that moment, she hadn't understood how much she wanted him to forgive her.

Silence fell, but it wasn't uncomfortable. They stood only a metre or so apart, the sun warming them both, neither speaking, until after a minute, he said, 'Tell me about your life.'

It was a command, and it made her laugh, despite the inherent danger in the question. After all, Annie was the biggest part of her life. How could she discuss her day-to-day existence without mentioning their daughter? And how could she bring up Annie until she understood him better? Until she knew how he'd react?

'My life is busy,' she said. 'I work long hours.'

'You never married?'

Her heart stammered. 'I'm only twenty-six,' she pointed out.

'Are you seeing anyone?'

She bit into her lower lip. 'After the way we kissed yesterday?'

He lifted his shoulders. 'We didn't have sex. It would hardly have been a massive betrayal.'

Her lips parted in surprise. 'No,' she said quickly, not meeting his eyes. 'I'm not seeing anyone. And if I was, I wouldn't have kissed you like that. I'm not quite so cavalier with my feelings are you are.'

His smile prickled at her heart. 'Peace offering, remember.'

'Maybe there's too much in our past to ever achieve peace?' she said softly, hoping that it wasn't true. They shared a daughter; for Annie's sake they needed to resolve their past.

'Perhaps peace is overrated,' he said, eyes boring into hers, warming her, teasing her, tempting her. She stared at him, every nerve ending in her body reverberating in recognition of what he was suggesting, of the truth in his words. She took an involuntary step backwards, gripping her cup more tightly.

'Thank you for the coffee,' she mumbled. 'I should—I need to go.'

'Coward,' he taunted softly, his smile sending her nerves into overdrive.

As she hurried across the courtyard, she heard his soft, mocking laugh and her insides squirmed with unmistakable desire—a desire she knew she had to conquer.

CHAPTER SIX

'COME WITH ME.'

She lifted her face to his as if awakening from a dream. 'What time is it?'

'Eight o'clock.'

'Eight o'clock at night?' She flicked a glance back to her computer screen. 'Wow. I didn't realise. I've been working.' She stood up with unconscious grace, rolling her head from side to side to ease the pressure in her neck. His eyes followed the gesture so she stopped abruptly. She'd been hiding in her room since their earlier exchange in the courtyard, terrified of how quickly he could wind her up and turn her insides to mush. She had to focus on the business side of things. 'Would you like to hear what I've come up with?'

'Not particularly.' His eyes held hers and desire sparked in her bloodstream.

Business, business, business.

'What can I do for you?'

His eyes bore into hers, slicing her with the heat of his gaze, and she shivered as a frisson of awareness travelled the length of her spine.

'I want to show you something.'

'What is it?'

He expelled a sigh. 'I did not say I want to *tell* you something. Come with me.'

His authority was compelling. 'Do I need shoes?'

'No.' And to her surprise, he held out his hand, staring at her impatiently.

She froze, the offered hand so much more than just a gesture. Her heart leaped into her throat and she looked down at his wrist, his fingers, with a sense that putting her own in his would be like sealing her fate—a fate she might not want to exist with, a fate she couldn't outrun.

Slowly, she moved closer, and then, of its own volition, her hand lifted, meeting his halfway. The moment they touched, an electrical current fizzed through her, so, startled, she turned to him.

'This won't take long.'

Did he feel it at all? Did he realise how even the air around them seemed to change when they touched?

He led her out of the house through yet another set of doors. 'I swear, after two days' exploring, I still can't get my bearings.'

'I'll give you a tour tomorrow.'

Her heart thundered.

Careful, Alicia. Once bitten, twice shy...

'Another peace offering?'

He flicked her a grin and her insides knotted together.

The grass was dewy underfoot, the evening air still sultry and warm, the day's heat refusing to budge despite the setting sun. She moved closer to him on autopilot, despite the warmth, and he held the line, so their bodies brushed as they walked. Each light brush of skin sent her pulse into overdrive and sparked a tangle of need in the pit of her stomach, so she was breathless by the time they reached the sand of the shoreline.

'There.' He pointed to a large stretch of grass that ran beside the sand.

'Your second option,' she said breathlessly, because it was perfect. But so, too, was the courtyard! 'Both stunning,' she said honestly. 'You'll have to choose which you like best.'

'Do you have a preference?'

'I won't be here,' she said, and she wasn't imagining the wistful tone to her voice. She covered it by plastering an overbright smile to her face. 'I suppose the house has more practical advantages, but there's no reason not to have sunset drinks here, at the water's edge. This could have a whole other theme. Whereas the dinner at the house could be more formal, with a classical band, this could be relaxed—a beachy, tropical party, with a percussion band to dance to.'

'Dancing?'

'What's a party without dancing?' she responded archly.

'I'll take your word for it.'

'Don't tell me you don't dance?'

'That surprises you? Did we ever dance back then?'

'No. There wasn't the opportunity.'

And then his other hand lifted to her cheek, cupping it, holding her still so he could inspect her better in the fading light of the day. His eyes trapped hers and it felt as though she were tipping off the edge of the earth. She was in a void with nothing and no one else—just Graciano and herself.

'I dance rarely.'

'I bet you're good at it.' She could have sewn her lips together!

'How much?'

'An actual wager?'

'Sure. Unless you're scared to lose?'

'I won't lose. I know you've got rhythm.'

His features showed scepticism. 'We'll see.'

'Okay. A hundred euros?'

'I was thinking more like a non-monetary wager.'

Her heart crashed into her ribs with the force of a jet engine. 'Such as?' The words were barely audible.

'If I win, you'll answer any question I have.'

Danger lurked. Annie was, as always, in the back of her mind. 'No.'

His eyes narrowed. 'Keeping secrets?'

She blinked down at the grass between them. 'I'll give you three questions,' she said unevenly. 'And I get to veto one of them.'

'You drive a hard bargain.'

'What do I get if I win?'

'What do you want?'

She felt heat stain her cheeks and looked away, embarrassed by how easy she was to read. 'The same deal. Three questions.'

'And a veto.'

'Fair enough.'

He dropped his hand to her other, capturing both. 'Are you ready?'

'What for?'

'To dance.'

'*With* me?' she squeaked.

'Did you think I was going to torture myself solo?'

But she was trembling from top to toe. How could she possibly dance with him? Alarm sirens blared but she couldn't heed them. He drew her into his body and she let him, his large frame wrapping around her, one hand in the small of her back, the other holding her hand close to their shoulders.

'There's no music,' she said as he began to move with, as she'd guessed, impeccable timing.

'There is the beat of the waves hitting the coast. The birds overhead. Listen, and you'll hear it.'

She turned her head, pressing her cheek to his chest so the fast beating of his heart added to the background song nature was weaving around them. He was right; there was music everywhere. She closed her eyes, breathing in, tasting his masculine, spiced scent, letting it flood her body with strength and need.

Time ceased to exist. They danced—for how long, she couldn't have said. For a long time, and not enough, their bodies enmeshed, their steps in perfect unison. The sun set and the stars shimmered, the night sky a perfect inky black overhead. Alicia felt the illicit pleasure of this moment, of being held by him as though it were normal, their bodies brushing together in the seemingly innocuous task of dancing, when really, magic was weaving around them, making them both want—need—so much more.

That need terrified her, and despite the nirvana of the moment, Alicia forced herself to stiffen in his arms, to stop swaying in time to the magical music he'd made her aware of and look up at him. All her futures, all her hopes, distilled into that one single look. She was standing on a precipice, a terrifying drop before her, and yet she moved closer to the edge, lifting a hand to his chest, fingers splayed against the fabric of his shirt.

'I win.' The words were husky, and the sting of tears made her throat hurt.

At sixteen, she'd wanted him with her whole heart. She'd never really recovered from that.

But he'd walked away, she reminded herself quickly. True, she'd failed to defend him the morning after her birthday, when Edward Griffiths had found them asleep in a field, limbs entwined, only a flimsy blanket for cover. But he'd disappeared, and when she'd tried to explain, to apologise, he'd refused to let her explain. He'd been so brutal in his rejection.

It had broken her heart.

It was still broken.

What other explanation was there for her celibacy since? She had told herself it was because of Annie, that being a single mother took all her focus, but that didn't explain her disgust at the idea of dating any other man. Graciano's rejection had left her terrified of experiencing that same pain again.

Yet here she was, dangerously close to him in every sense, her heart beating a frantic, desperate tattoo, all for him. She knew she had to stay away, or at least harden her heart before it could hurt anew, but closeness was addictive, and suddenly, Alicia was tired of fighting herself.

'I think we should call it a draw.'

She lifted a brow, her pulse tripping over itself. 'I'm not sure that's fair.'

'Dancing is subjective.'

'So you entrapped me in a bet I could never truly win?'

His smile was sheer arrogant masculinity. 'I don't like to lose.'

Her stomach squeezed. Conscious of how she stood, in the circle of his arms, she pulled back, the walls of her world splintering, but she was determined not to let them shatter completely. There was a secret she held deep inside her, a secret she'd sworn she'd keep. But the longer she spent with Graciano, the more at risk that secret became—the more she wanted to tell him everything.

Fear sliced through her. She couldn't even imagine how Graciano would react to the news that he was the father to a nine-year-old girl. Just the idea of having that conversation drained all the colour from her face and she had to turn away from him abruptly, to face the ocean, to hide the response from him.

She alone had borne the consequences of the night they'd shared, and that had seemed right. After all, it had never been 'just sex' for her, which meant their baby was not a burden, despite what it had cost Alicia—despite the way a bomb had blown up in her life.

Her decision-making had been sound, but standing beside him now, it felt like a grenade with the ring pulled. She didn't know how to stave off the devastating explosion.

'Okay. You go first,' she said, to buy for time, needing to distract him from the way the past was rushing at her, haunting her, terrorising her.

'Tell me about your life.'

'That's not a question.'

'No. I suppose it's not.'

A small smile lifted her lips. 'Want to try again?'

He considered that a moment. 'Have you always wanted to work in events?'

Alicia's lips pulled to the side. 'I've always been organised—'

'I remember.'

His interruption did something funny to her tummy, making it twist and tighten. 'As for events, it was a…friend…who suggested I pursue this career.'

'A friend?'

She nodded softly. 'Diane's sister worked in events, and got me a job at the palace. It was a baptism by fire, but so rewarding. I learned so much.'

'You left, though.'

'Yes.' She nodded. Annie had been in nursery school, and Alicia had needed something with more flexibility. 'The hours were incredibly long, and a job came up in the charity. The work environment is very flexible, and incredibly rewarding. It was a good fit.'

'And you've done very well for the charity.'

'Is that another question?'

'An observation. Your services were hotly contested.'

'Well, yes, but no one had quite the deep pockets you do.'

He shrugged.

'Why did you bid on me, Graciano?'

'To organise—'

'No.' She bit down on her lip. 'You have people to organise events. You have whole departments. Why me? Why now?' Her voice shook a little on the last question.

His nostrils flared as he exhaled, eyes roaming her face, and then he moved closer, so they stood toe to toe, staring at each other. 'It was a spontaneous decision.'

'A very expensive one.'

He dipped his head in agreement.

It didn't make any sense.

'Have you thought about me?'

'What do you mean?'

'Since you left my father's. Have you thought about me?'

'Yes.' The tone of his voice left her in little doubt: those thoughts were not good.

'I have another question.'

'I've lost count of how many you've asked.'

'Does it matter?'

The air around them crackled. She wondered if he was going to argue with her, but he stayed silent, waiting.

'Have you ever been in love?' The question was out of her mouth before she could think it through, before she analysed how much it revealed about her. Before she debated whether she even wanted to hear the answer. But she held her breath, waiting, staring up at him, analysing his response.

He dropped his hand away and turned to face the ocean. His dark eyes scanned the frothy waves, the stars. 'Veto.'

She sucked in a shaky breath and mirrored his posture, turning to face the sea. Far across the rolling water, mainland Spain stood sentinel, its rich history and tapestry the place Alicia had felt most at home. She closed her eyes against the pain of that, against the devastating body blow of loss.

'It's not a hard question.'

'The ability to use a veto isn't dependent on the difficulty of answering.'

She ground her teeth together. 'You're not playing the game properly.'

'You're right. Let me answer your earlier question better, then. You asked why I brought you here.'

She held her breath, staring at him.

He studied her right back, appraising, and she felt a rush of emotions swamping her, drowning her, so she struggled to stay standing. Perhaps he realised, because a moment later his hand came around her back, supporting her, pressing her forward, no longer in an invitation to dance but in an embrace that made the nerve endings in her body vibrate furiously.

'And?' she whispered, glad for his support.

'I was curious about you.'

'Angry with me?' She pushed, because she'd felt it humming off him in waves that night at the charity ball.

'It was ten years ago,' he pointed out with a voice that was all reason and calm.

'You said you'd be honest.'

Silence whipped the air between them, followed by a sharp hiss of breath between his teeth. 'I was angry,' he agreed after a beat. '*Si*. I was made to feel worthless for a long time, by many people. Until I met you, no one had ever seen value in me. No one had ever wanted me.'

Her heart twisted painfully in her chest.

'But *you* wanted me. I didn't realise how much I cared for your good opinion until it was wrenched away. Do you remember what he said? What he accused me of? The threats he made? And I turned to you, looking for support, sure that you would help me make him understand. You were silent. Worse, you moved to him, put your hand on his arm. I was so angry with myself. I had let down my guard with you. I'd let myself need someone for the first time in my life. I'd let myself believe...'

'You were right to believe,' she whispered, the words tortured, her throat heavy with emotion. 'My father made the situation untenable, but that didn't change how I felt. I was only sixteen, Graciano. Just a girl.'

'Not when you were with me.'

'No.' A wistful smile twisted her lips. There was so much water under the bridge. 'With you, I felt like a woman.'

'I left Seville and swore I would never let another person have the kind of power over me that you did that summer. I lost myself in you, *querida*, and it's a mistake I've never since repeated.'

Her heart soared even when a rock dropped

through her body, landing low in her gut. 'But when I called to apologise—'

'I'd learned my lesson,' he said with a lift of his shoulders. 'You were dangerous. Quicksand. When I was around you, I wanted only you. I forgot about my brother, my plans for my future, my desire to succeed. There was only you.' His lips tightened into a grimace. 'I was too selfish to allow for that.'

Her eyes swept shut at his admission. Was that it? Would their relationship have been doomed to fail anyway? He was an ambitious man—his success proved that—so perhaps he would have moved on anyway, rather than risk his ambitions failing.

'So you told me you'd moved on—'

'Oh, no, Alicia. I didn't lie to you.'

Her chest panged.

'I wanted to put you from my mind, to erase you from my body. Sex seemed like the most expedient way.'

'Did it work?' she challenged, tilting her chin defiantly to cover the shattering of her heart.

'Yes.' His eyes glittered with a challenge when they locked to hers. Her skin flushed hot and cold.

'That still doesn't explain why you brought me here,' she said unevenly. 'If you were angry, why not ignore me? Leave without speaking to me?'

'Where's the fun in that?'

She flinched but didn't back down, didn't move away. 'Where's the fun in this?'

'Are you not enjoying yourself?'

Her stomach somersaulted through her. She felt as though she were on a medieval torture device; at the same time, she couldn't imagine walking away from Graciano at the end of this week and never seeing him again. It would be like losing a limb.

'I'm here to work,' she said quietly.

'And did you come here thinking it would all be about work? Or were you hoping…?' He let the question dangle in the air between them.

'I didn't even know if you'd be here,' she said, truthfully. 'I had no idea what to expect.'

He paused. 'Nor did I.'

Frustration zipped through her—frustration with him, their past, their circumstances, with how much she wanted him and how strongly she knew she should fight that. 'Are you playing games with me?'

She saw the response in his eyes, his expression, the minute changes before he quickly resumed a mask of total control.

'To what end?'

'I don't know. To punish me?'

'Revenge?' he prompted.

'Yes.'

'It did occur to me.'

She shivered at the bald acknowledgement. 'That's why I'm here? So you can sleep with me and make me…what? Love you?'

'I don't want your love,' he dismissed quickly.

'But you do want me to want you,' she said after a heavy pause. 'You know what you do to me, how you make me feel. You brought me here to capitalise on that, to seduce me. And then what?'

He was silent, but his jaw was locked, and she felt his emotions, dark and…ashamed? Angry?

'I intended to, yes. I wanted to make you mine, for this week, to make you forget about any other man you've been with, to make you admit you wanted me like you want air. There is unfinished business between us, Alicia.' He took a step backwards from her then, and the moon pierced her with a fine, silver blade. 'But the truth is, that one night we were together was a lifetime ago. Just like you said—ancient history. Let's leave it where it belongs—in the past.' And with that, he spun on his heel and began to walk back towards the house.

CHAPTER SEVEN

'DON'T YOU WALK away from me,' she shouted, with far more command than she felt. 'You're the one who brought me to this island, who paid a fortune to secure my time. Don't turn your back when you don't like the way the conversation's going.'

'That's not it,' he snapped over his shoulder.

'Isn't it?' She scrambled after him, propelled by frustration.

'What do you want from me?' he muttered, the words only barely audible. She moved faster, until she was almost level with him, then reached out and caught his wrist.

'Damn you!'

The sound of their breathing, each as frantic as the other, filled the air, and then he made a gruff, growling sound and freed his wrist, only so he could wrap his arms around her and yank her body to his, pulling her to him. 'Your father robbed us both of a chance to explore this,' he said, but his voice was quiet, as though he was speaking to himself more than her. 'That's why it feels as though there's something unfinished between us. That's why there's this compulsion.

We need to get it out of our system, to let it burn out, and then we can move on.'

Move on. It all made sense, but his words had a brutal resonance that made her heart feel bruised and heavy, and she didn't know why.

The question formed in her mind—a barbed, painful thought she couldn't contemplate— because she knew now, beyond a shadow of a doubt, that her daughter deserved better than this.

'Graciano,' she said, with urgency. She wasn't ready to tell him about Annie, but she did need some kind of absolution. 'I was angry, too. So angry. I was only sixteen, and you were the best friend I'd ever had.'

He made a noise of disbelief. She ignored it.

'If I let you down, then you did the same to me. I needed you. I needed you...'

He kissed her then, the kiss angry and gentle, a kiss of mastery and promise, a kiss designed to silence her sad pleas. He pulled her to the ground, the grass beneath them cool and dewy in the evening air, his weight on her a drugging delight. His hands moved over her quickly, discarding her clothes with impatience while he kissed her, crushing her lips, moving his hips, promising her, silently, always, of the pleasures to come.

Naked beneath him, she arched her back, then

lifted up, seeking him once more, but he stayed where he was, still clothed, staring down at her. His eyes held hers until her heart exploded and she had to close the distance between them and kiss him to stop from saying three words that were pulsing around her mind without any anchor point in reality. She didn't *love* him. She'd *loved* him, once, a long, long time ago, as a teenager who'd had no inkling about life and people and loyalty and what love really even meant.

Kissing him was simple, though. When they kissed, and touched, no explanation was necessary. She needed no time to analyse what any of it meant; it was written in the stars. She said his name over again, the syllables husky and exotic beneath the Mediterranean moonlight, the taste in her mouth building like an incantation, a spell over both, over this glorious bay and all that was here on this island.

He ripped off his shirt, discarding it at their sides, his chest moving powerfully with each breath. The moonlight landed like a shaft across his torso, catching words that ran in cursive script just beneath his heart. She lifted a finger, chasing them, saying them aloud so they washed through the air, adding weight to the incantation of his name.

'*Que cada palo aguante su vela.*' They were

beautiful words, though she didn't understand their literal meaning.

'*Si*,' he agreed, though, and then he was moving over her, kicking out of his shoes as her hands found the button of his trousers and unfastened it, then pushed them down, hungry for him, terrified of her need, but unwilling—unable—to stop.

Ten years ago, their coming together had been tentative and gentle—an exploration, an awakening—but now, a decade's worth of need pulsed through them like a live wire, driving her hands so she stripped him naked as he pushed out of his trousers, working together to liberate him, needing him with the power of a thousand suns.

'Please,' she groaned to underscore her desperation and he laughed, a low, growling sound that pulsed in her belly, but then he stopped, moving over her, his face just an inch from hers.

'We can't do this.'

Something dropped inside of her. A weight. A loss. An ache spread. 'What do you mean?'

'I don't have a condom.'

'Oh, my God.' She lifted a hand to his chest, shocked that she could have been so caught up in the moment she'd forgotten the simple precaution. Even that night, he'd used one—though it hadn't stopped her from falling pregnant.

'I never don't use protection,' he said through ground teeth, lips clenched, and then he cursed, the word vibrating around them, and she flinched, not from the word itself but from the force of his disappointment—a perfect echo of her own.

'No,' she groaned, squeezing her eyes shut, trembling with her need. In that moment, she would almost have risked another child simply for the exquisite pleasure of knowing his possession once more. 'I can't believe it.'

'I'm not—I'm sure—' But what could she say? That she was sure they wouldn't fall pregnant? When the impossible had already happened despite them using protection?

'I won't take the risk.'

Her heart skipped, because his protestations showed how devoutly he wanted to avoid the complication of a pregnancy.

'Are you on the pill?'

Oh, she wished she was, but why would she have been? Slowly, she shook her head. 'I'm not in the habit of this kind of thing.' She dropped her gaze between them, hating how much that revealed to him, hating how unsophisticated and inexperienced she was. But he moved quickly, his mouth finding hers and kissing her until she wasn't thinking straight and her hips were moving, silently inviting him to take her, to become one with her. His hand moved between her legs while he kissed her with his own desperate hunger, his fingers finding the sensitive cluster of nerve endings and brushing over them so she cried out into his mouth, the noise harsh and afraid. Pleasures almost unknown to Alicia began to cut through her like blades of lightning, arcing from the centre of her womanhood through every cell in her body until she was a trembling mess beneath him.

He struck a finger inside of her and she jolted off the ground at the invasion, surprising and welcoming, and he laughed again, but there was restraint to it, as if he was just holding on to his own sanity. With no experience to guide her, only instincts, her hands moved across his body, feeling the sculptured lines of his abdomen before running lower, to the hardness of his arousal. He swore as she gripped him in the palms of her hands, as he throbbed and swore again. Then he moved his own hand faster, and she was no longer capable of moving or hearing or speaking. She was on fire, burning from the inside out, every part of her aflame. She whimpered into his mouth, against his cheek, and then, as the heat of her orgasm detonated all through her, she cried his name into the night sky and arched her back, utterly, totally overcome by the strength of her pleasure, but also, regardless, by her need for him.

He watched her come back to earth, his control considerably frayed at the edges given the way her hands were spasmodically clutching his length, her grip animalistic and primal, desperate and possessive, her face scrunched up in pleasure and his body desperate to feel her, to be inside her. He moved his hands to her hips, then higher to cup her breasts, so she released her grip on him and lay back on the grass, staring at his face, frowning, as though she'd never seen him before.

Something hummed in the air between them— words unspoken, a confession—and he wondered. He felt a weight inside of her, felt an ache he couldn't fathom, and so he kissed her slowly, wanting to erase the frown, wanting to taste her, to feel her.

Ten years ago, when he'd made love to her— taken her innocence in a field not dissimilar to this one, their backs then on a picnic rug rather than the grass—he'd felt a connection unlike anything he'd ever known. Before that, he'd had sex. But with Alicia, it had been a connection of their souls, a frighteningly intimate experience that had changed him.

He'd never known a feeling like it since, and he couldn't help but wonder… Would it be like that again now? Even watching as she came had pulled at a piece of him, unravelling bonds he'd formed many years earlier, a tightness in his chest that had served him well.

But this was just an itch he needed to scratch, like he'd said. They had unfinished business. The sooner they finished it and could move on, the better.

He lifted her just as he had the first day she'd arrived and twisted her ankle, holding her naked body against his chest as they approached the house, and she was too alive with nerves and anticipation to think clearly. Only as he shouldered the doors in, she startled, putting a hand on his shoulder. 'Isabella,' she reminded him anxiously, looking around.

'Is nowhere to be seen.' But he moved faster, and rather than entering the courtyard, he turned right and took a set of stairs that led to a part of the house she hadn't explored. When he shouldered in the door to his bedroom, her heart splintered apart, just as she'd known it would, to be crossing this threshold of intimacy, to be entering his private sanctuary.

Her senses were overloaded. The room was large, with a huge bed against one wall, darkly wooded side tables and a leather sofa across the space. A television hung above a fireplace, and two narrow doors marked the edge of the room—one leading to a wardrobe, she guessed, the other, a bathroom, going from the tiles she could see on the floor. The artwork on the walls was bold and modern, and the curtains that hung were dark navy. Everything in here was overtly masculine, including a lingering aroma of cologne that made her groan softly.

He placed her on the edge of the bed and stood back, regarding her slowly. 'Are you sure you want this?' he demanded, watching her, his face terse, his eyes showing impatience.

She was tempted to toy with him, to tease him, but her desire was too oversized, and their shared past and pain too mighty to be treated frivolously.

'Yes.' A simple answer that had him moving quickly to his bedside table and opening a drawer, removing a line of condoms and perforating one from the rest before slicing it across the top. She watched, riveted, as he unfurled it over his length, then came back to her, standing over her, chest heaving so her eyes fell first to his tattoo then lower, to his arousal. She gasped, because he was so very large and tantalising that her skin lifted in goosebumps and she felt a strange heat spool between her legs.

'I want you,' she insisted again, lifting a hand to reach for him, but that wasn't necessary. Graciano was already moving, his body nudging her backwards on the bed. She wriggled up into the centre and he chased her, his mouth finding hers and claiming it as his knee nudged her legs apart, and his body pressed down on hers, every soft curve of her against all his hard planes.

She trembled with the promise of what was to come, with the force of her need. His hands caught hers, lacing their fingers together, holding them to the side, and she squirmed beneath him, trying, needing, to feel him inside.

His throaty laugh sent goosebumps all over her.

She arched her back and he moved a hand to her thigh, lifting it this time, pushing it aside, before nudging his tip at her entrance, teasing her so she moaned and tried to take him deeper, but Graciano was in complete control. Or was he? When she peeked at his face, she saw the effort that control was taking, his features carved from steel, his skin ashen.

'I want you,' she repeated, like a prayer, then bit down on her lip as finally he thrust into her, once, hard, fast, and she exploded, his possession unique and perfect, barriers that only he had breached in the past, only once, broken again, her muscles so tight around him, squeezing him so she cried out as the beginning of an orgasm began to froth in her fingertips, to spread through every cell in her body.

'*Cristo*, you're so tight,' he ground out, moving his mouth to her neck and sucking her flesh there, his stubble a delightful pleasure-pain offset by the sweetness of his lips and tongue, the warmth of his breath. Then he was dragging across her décolletage, moving harder, deeper, until she couldn't see straight and thought she might pass out from pleasure.

She tilted off the edge of the earth, no longer human, no longer recognisable, grabbing hold of his shoulders as she spun away from any form of reality, and he whispered words in her ears, Spanish words that she couldn't understand properly but adored nonetheless. A moment later, while she was still grappling with the waves of her pleasure, the turbulence rocking her, he began to move once more, and she realised how much of himself he'd been holding back the first time, because this was *all* of him, everything, so much so that she bucked and twisted and cried out in delirium as new pleasures spread through her and she was barely human.

Again she felt the world slip away from her, mania driving her to the edge of reason and sense, and this time he was with her, his guttural cry as he exploded only adding to the intensity of her pleasure, the perfection of that moment.

She sobbed as he lay on top of her, their hearts

racing, his arousal jerking inside of her as he rode his own wave of euphoria, his breath brushing her cheek.

A single tear rolled down her cheek, landing between them, so Graciano shifted, frowning as he lifted up to look at her. His eyes scanned hers, worry in their depths, but then he smiled, a smile that creased the corners of his eyes and made her heart do a strange twisty looping. *This* was her Graciano as he'd been then, without all the cynicism and anger, without the boundaries he'd been forced to build around himself except when they were together.

He rolled away from her onto his back, separating them so her body reacted with a violent protest, not wanting him to be apart from her even when she knew, with every fibre of her being, that they would be together again. There was no way they could fight that. Not for the rest of this week. Beyond that, their futures were apart, but here, now, being together was imperative.

They lay side by side for a long time, rushed breathing eventually slowing, her eyes drying, sense returning. There were no regrets.

'That was...' She couldn't think of an appropriate word.

'Nice?' he interjected, teasing a little.

'I suppose it was,' she agreed, grinning.

'*Nice?*' he repeated, with mock outrage. 'I really hope not.'

'Is there something wrong with *nice*?'

'It's a little bland for what we just did.'

She laughed softly, then turned to face him. It was a mistake. Her heart lurched and the world tipped off its axis completely. Fresh tears filmed her eyes. She flipped onto her back once more, staring at the ceiling; it was far safer.

'What is it?'

How could she answer that? How could she tell him how sad she felt for what they'd lost? The chance to be together, to be a family, the chance to know one another properly, beyond that night they'd shared?

She'd been bullied into giving him up. Her love for him had been manipulated by a father who couldn't bear to lose control of his 'good' little daughter.

She ground her teeth together, the past a prickly patch to contemplate. 'What does this mean?' she asked, changing the subject as she ran her finger over the tattoo on his chest.

He hesitated, as though he wasn't going to answer. 'It means, "May every mast hold its own sail."'

She pulled her lips to one side. 'I don't get it.'

'On a ship, each mast holds a sail of its own. That sail fills with wind, and the wind directs it. We make choices, those choices have consequences.'

Her heart skipped a beat. 'Every mast has its own sail,' she repeated, thinking of her own choices, thinking of Annie, a lump in her throat.

'When did you get it?'

'Years ago.'

She rolled her eyes. 'Two years ago, five years ago, ten years ago?' Her throat went dry as she offered the last suggestion.

'About eight, I think. I can't quite remember.'

'Why did you choose it?'

'I like the expression,' he said with a shrug, as though it barely mattered. 'It's something my father used to say.'

That pricked her attention. Only once, back then, had he referred to his real family, referencing deceased parents and a younger brother. She knew he didn't like to talk of them, so hearing the casual reference to his father had her pushing up onto her elbow, looking at him with more care. 'Tell me about him.'

His eyes shuttered. She'd pushed it too far. He wouldn't speak.

Her sigh was soft—an acceptance of his boundaries, of his desire to keep that part of his life locked up. 'My own father is still in Seville, you know,' she said after a pause, lifting a finger and absentmindedly tracing the tattoo.

'I wasn't aware.' There was a coldness in his tone, but she understood it.

'He's no longer involved in the church, but his life is there now.'

'Not with you?'

'I haven't seen him in a long time.'

She felt his chest still, as though he were holding his breath.

'A month after you left, he sent me to England.'

'Sent you? Without him?'

She nodded.

Graciano's eyes flicked to hers, a thousand questions in them. 'How did you feel about that?'

She frowned. 'Better not to ask how I felt then. Now, I'm glad he sent me away,' she said firmly, with defiance. 'It was the right decision.'

'You were sixteen. He was your only family.'

'Not quite. I lived with my grandmother—his mother.'

'Even then, you didn't see him?'

The colour had drained from her face. 'He wouldn't see me,' she said quietly.

Graciano caught her hand, holding it still on his chest. 'Because of me?'

'Because of us,' she said softly, on a gentle sob. 'Because of what we did.'

He swore under his breath. 'You were a teenager. You made a mistake.'

'He didn't raise me to make mistakes. He

didn't raise me to sin,' she corrected with vehemence. 'What we did was a crime in the eyes of the Lord. His words, not mine.'

'And so he threw you out?'

'Not onto the streets, as he did you,' she said angrily.

'It was just one night,' he said with a shake of his head, clearly not realising how that evaluation cut her. 'What about forgiveness?'

'I have come to understand that my father talked the talk but didn't walk the walk. His faith is skin-deep.'

'I have had the same reflection.'

Their eyes met and something hummed between them—a shared understanding.

'Why did you bother telling him the truth about us? I had already left, with no intention of coming back.'

She bit down on her lip. Even now, ten years later, it still stung. 'I...'

'Be honest,' he insisted, after she hesitated.

Alicia nodded. 'I couldn't bear for him to think what he did of you. I couldn't bear the thought of him...telling anyone...what he believed you'd done. I didn't want what we'd shared to be sullied in that way. You deserved so much better.'

He lifted a hand to her cheek, stroking it gently. 'I was wrong about you. All these years, I thought you a coward.'

Her heart soared, but she didn't deserve his praise. Annie was always there, in the back of her mind, a secret she'd kept to protect Graciano, but now, as an adult, she realised how greatly she'd deprived him.

'My own father was an excellent man,' he said into the silence so her stomach twisted and she moved closer unconsciously. 'I was only seven when he died, but my memories of him—and my parents—are strong. Perhaps loss sharpened them?'

She stayed quiet, waiting, knowing that her silence would encourage more confidences than probing questions.

'He was a lawyer. As a child, I knew only that he worked hard and always carried a heavy brief-case. Now, I have more information. He was a family lawyer, a working legal aid for children. My mother was a doctor.' His smile was regretful. 'She didn't work when we were young, but she'd just started talking about going back. They sometimes fought about it.'

'He didn't want her to work?'

'I suppose not. My memories of the details there aren't clear. She was very beautiful,' he said, distracted. 'She had long, dark hair that she would loop into a bun high on her head every day. Then each night, she would sit cross-legged on the sofa and pull out the pins, one by one, until it unfurled like a waterfall over one shoulder. My father would comb it with his fingers, and she'd purr like a cat.'

His smile was, strangely for Graciano, almost self-conscious. 'It's odd, the things we remember. Some memories like that are locked in my brain. I can replay them on cue, like a TV show. Others are grainier.'

She weaved their fingers together, dragging his hand to her lips and pressing a kiss against it.

'I know she used to read to my brother and me every night, but I cannot ever remember which books—only the sensation of my brother's little body being curled up at my side and my mother perched beside us, my eyes growing heavy even when I was determined to stay awake, her hand brushing my forehead as I fell asleep. Fragments of memories, impressions of feelings.'

'It sounds like you were very loved.'

'They were good parents,' he said with a small nod. 'They taught me the importance of family.'

'Your brother... Did he...?' She let the question hang in the air.

'No. He survived the crash, but afterwards, we were separated.'

Her brow was quizzical. 'What do you mean?'

'He was badly injured. I was not. I had to be

put into foster placement immediately. I saw him in hospital once, but not again—he was too ill. I thought I'd see him when he was better, but days turned into weeks and weeks into months. My foster parents couldn't afford to care for another child. A different home was found for him.'

Alicia gasped. 'That's awful. Could you see him at least?'

'No.' He squeezed her hand. 'Perhaps if a lawyer like my father had been involved, but neither foster parent welcomed the contact. After three months, I was moved to a different home, and then another.' He stood abruptly, striding naked across the room to a tall chest of drawers. He hesitated a moment, then opened a small drawer at the top and removed a piece of paper, crossed the room and handed it to her. 'This is all I had.'

She sat up, taking the photo from him and cradling it in her palm. It was aged, and had obviously been well loved. Her eyes roamed the faces staring back at her: a man who was slender and smiling, wearing a buttoned shirt with jeans and dark hair shoulder length, and two little boys— Graciano with his knees up under his chin, a look of concentration on his face, and his baby brother, with chubby cheeks and a silly grin.

So he'd been serious even before the accident, before the foster care system, before life on the streets?

The photo made her smile, even as it formed a heavy notch in her belly, because how could she ignore the woman in the photo? A woman just as Graciano had described: very beautiful, with silky dark hair and soulful eyes, a woman who was so familiar to her, so achingly known and loved. This was Annie's grandmother—but it could have been Annie. Their eyes, their smiles, their hair. This was Annie's family.

She lifted her spare hand to her mouth and pressed her fingertips there, the heaviness of her betrayal landing like a thud in the centre of her chest.

'As a child in the foster system, you are somewhat powerless. I could do nothing to find Diego. But I remembered my father's voice. Again and again, when we were boys, he would say to me, "He's your brother. It's your job to take care of him." I never forgot that.'

Emotion weighed down on her. She nodded, not trusting herself to speak.

'When I was older, one of my social workers took the time to look into it for me. I was told he'd been adopted by Americans. I don't know if it's true or not. Adoption records are sealed, but perhaps.'

'That's devastating for you. Surely now there must be something—'

'I hired an investigator, some years ago,' he

said, closing down on her, the conversation growing too heavy, too frustrating for him. 'I have learned a little more about his life after the accident, before his adoption, but nothing after.'

'Hire a different investigator,' she advised swiftly. 'There *must* be something.'

'Believe me, I've tried. It's as though he's been erased. I do not know where he went, and for years, I lived with the guilt of having let down my father.'

'Your father wouldn't blame you for this,' she assured him quickly. 'None of it is your fault. It seems barbaric to me that any foster agency would split two brothers...'

'Yes,' he said after a beat. 'It is barbaric. You're right.'

But wasn't she just as bad? After all, she'd split Graciano from his daughter. It was hard to look at him without feeling that monumental burden of guilt.

'Why did you leave foster care?'

Again, she felt him closing down. 'I had several bad placements in a row. I was fourteen by then. Life on the streets seemed more appealing.'

'And was it?'

He contemplated that. 'I was my own man.'

'But surely in foster care you at least had a bed, a roof, some food...'

'Everything has a price, Alicia. I preferred to pay mine on the streets.'

It was all so sad. She ached for the life he'd experienced, for what he'd gone through.

'What about an estate?' she murmured, the idea occurring to her out of nowhere. 'Surely your parents had a home, savings, things that could have saved you from living rough.'

'In fact, they did,' he said quietly. 'Unfortunately, I didn't know about it until after I'd made enough money of my own to pay someone to look into it for me.'

She gasped with indignation. 'But surely that should have gone to you.'

'Probably. By the time I learned of the inheritance, which was held in trust for us jointly, I didn't need it. I have saved it for my brother. I don't know how he's living, whether life has been kind to him, but if he wants it, it's his.'

'I'm sure you'll find him,' she said, her words ringing with confidence. 'People don't just disappear into thin air.'

'I would simply like to know he's happy,' Graciano said, moving so that he could see the photo. 'As boys, we were very close. I adored him. It's strange that we're not in each other's lives now.'

She handed the photo back, feeling stung and uncertain. Nothing made sense. The words he'd just used were exactly how she felt about Graciano. She'd loved him so much ten years ago. How often had she thought of him since? Every day. Every damned day. And she'd thought that was because of Annie, but looking at him now, she was no longer convinced. It was Graciano she'd missed. Graciano she'd wanted.

The feeling that she was adrift in a churning sea only seemed to be getting worse, and she had no idea if there was an anchor or life vest to save her.

He thought she was asleep, but then she moved, pinning him with those assessing, intelligent eyes and something stirred in his gut—something long forgotten.

'Graciano.' She pressed a hand to his chest, then yawned, her eyes heavy. 'Before, when we were—'

'Having sex,' he provided, amused that even after sleeping together again and again, she couldn't form the words.

'No, before that. Outside.'

He waited, watching.

She seemed to be wading through sleep and thought, concentrating hard. 'We didn't have protection. Is that—are you—'

He frowned, not following; Alicia's expression showed frustration. 'You don't...'

'What are you trying to ask?' he asked, but with a soft laugh, lifting her hand and pressing it to his lips, a sinking feeling forming in the pit of his gut.

'Children,' she said quickly, not meeting his eyes. 'You don't want children?'

His brows shot up. 'Do *you* want children?'

She focused on the tattoo scrawled across his chest. 'You seemed disgusted by the idea.'

'No. Not disgusted,' he corrected, searching for a better way to describe how he felt. 'Adamantly opposed,' he settled on eventually.

Alicia's face was impossible to read, her eyes shielded from him by her determined focus on his chest. On the one hand, he was flattered. On the other, he wanted to see, to understand—to know what she was feeling. Danger perforated his lungs, making breathing difficult. He knew he should get out of bed, but he wasn't strong enough. Not then.

He'd been in the wilderness a long time; for now, he just wanted to enjoy the strange sensation that he'd come home, without analysing why that was problematic.

'Why?'

Her small-voiced question took a moment to understand. He'd forgotten what they were talking about. But how to answer? How to explain the hole that opened up inside his chest when he'd lost his family so many years ago? As a teenager, he'd known he'd never have a family. He was a loner, through and through. In fact, the only time he'd doubted that decision, that deeply held knowledge, was that one summer, what felt like a lifetime ago, in Seville.

'They're disgusting,' he said, flippantly. 'Tiny hands, sticky fingers.'

'I'm serious,' she said, blinking up at him so something jolted in his chest.

'So am I. Snotty noses. Do I really need to elaborate?'

'But your own children,' she said after a beat. 'Surely you've thought about it?'

'No,' he said firmly. 'That's one decision I've never doubted.' He didn't know why, but he couldn't admit the truth to Alicia—that as a boy of eighteen, when they'd met and he'd felt like maybe he wasn't a loner after all, he'd imagined a future rich with all the things so many people aspired to. That Alicia had made him doubt his desire to be solitary and truly independent.

But he'd been wrong then—there was no sense owning those feelings now.

'My family died when I was just a boy—I have never wanted another family. I have never wanted that for myself.'

He waited for her to say something else, but her eyes were closed, her body still, and he let her sleep, or feign sleep, because the silence suited him, too.

CHAPTER EIGHT

IT TOOK A MOMENT, and considerable skill, to coax his arm out from under Alicia without waking her, to slide from the bed slowly, gently, then stand, taking a few beats to stare down at her and reassure himself she was still asleep. After all, they'd had a disturbed night, punctuated by passion when their chemistry had sparked between them and demanded indulgence. He'd reached for her, or she'd reached for him, and the next moment, they'd been kissing, exploring one another, making love as though it were their lifeblood.

Her body was now as familiar to him as his own, and yet, she was still a mystery.

He stiffened, remember the words she'd spoken the night before describing her father's rejection of her, and a dark anger consumed him completely, forcing him away from the edge of the bed and away from Alicia, lest he make some kind of noise in response to the emotions rolling through him.

The truth was, minister Edward Griffiths was a total *bastardo*.

But why hadn't Graciano anticipated there would be consequences for Alicia? He grabbed some boxer shorts, then strode from the room, shutting the door gently before moving down the hallway towards the central stairs, while deep in thought.

The unpalatable truth was that he'd been so focused on himself he hadn't thought about Alicia, beyond how disappointed he'd been in her—how angry, how all his hopes and feelings and barely acknowledged future aspirations had been destroyed. That anger had prevented him from predicting the likelihood that she would go to her father with the truth. He hadn't foreseen that.

Now he wondered how that was possible. He'd spent months that summer watching her, admiring her, understanding her. She wasn't like anyone he'd ever met. She didn't judge him; she didn't care about his background. She was the first person in his life who really saw *him*, and wanted *him*. It was those very traits that had made her rejection sting all the worse. She'd brought him out into the light and then turned it off, and he'd been determined not to forgive her for that—but even when, as it turned out, she hadn't deserved a decade of his scorn?

He stopped in the kitchen, pressing his palms to the bench in a physical response to that. Snatches of that morning came into his mind, memories he'd spent a decade trying to ignore.

Edward Griffiths shouting. *You took advantage of my daughter! You raped her!*

And Alicia, silent, eyes to the floor, face ashen. He'd waited for her to interject. To say *anything*.

Get the hell off my property. If I ever see you again, I'll call the police. Hell, I'll call them right now.

And then Edward had put his arm around Alicia and led her away. They'd walked off, side by side, a team, Alicia's loyalty made oh so obvious by her choice to stay silent, to walk with Edward.

Graciano wasn't an idiot, though. His experiences had made him particularly demanding of fidelity, unable to forgive disloyalty. It was possible he'd expected more than any sixteen-year-old girl, who was alone in the world besides her father, could deliver. But he was sure she'd looked at him with coldness that morning. He'd felt her rejection—it had turned his blood to ice—but what if he'd been wrong? What if that had been fear of her father? His gut twisted at that new idea.

He made a coffee, then slipped out of the kitchen before anyone could appear and interrupt. He needed to be alone to reflect on the fact that last night had shifted something inside of him—something he'd held on to for a long time. Parameters that had defined his existence, that had been established for his safety and protection, were moving without his consent.

He took a long drink of his coffee, the first sip of the morning always a balm, then moved out into the garden, his eyes instinctively gravitating to the flat piece of land down by the sea. Without any forethought he moved there, legs long, carrying him with ease over the ground he knew so well, mind running over the predicament he found himself in.

He wasn't a foolish eighteen-year-old any more, under her spell for the first time, but nor was he blind to the problems that would arise if he let them become more entangled. His life was predicated on being alone, on being able to walk away from anyone and anything at any time. It was easy to exist in a world with tragedy and unfairness if one didn't develop attachments. If one didn't love.

The accident would not have destroyed him the way it did if he'd loved his parents and brother less. If his heart had been more under his control, he wouldn't have known that deep, gaping pain.

And again, as an eighteen-year-old, when Alicia's father had thrown him out…

Being alone was now his preferred mode of living, and Alicia was a grave threat to that. Or she would be, if he didn't continue to exercise total control in all their interactions—if he let himself forget that she would be leaving in a matter of days, if he let himself dream, for even a moment, that there could be a future for them… The whole point of having her here was to prove—to himself and her—that he could control his desire for her, that he could walk away on his own terms.

He finished his coffee, then bent down to retrieve her clothes from the night before, his hand fisting around the soft, dewy fabric before breathing in deeply and smelling her scent, sweet like vanilla. His gut rolled. There would be no future. Even though she'd explained her version of what had happened back then, it didn't change Graciano's reality.

Twice in his life, Graciano had known the god-awful pain of having had the rug pulled out from under him, the discombobulating certainty that his life was altered for ever and that he was powerless to contain that—once, when the car accident had taken his parents and brother from him, and again, when he'd known he'd lost Alicia. It was a pain he'd never open himself up to again. He would never allow himself to be destroyed like that again; he wasn't sure he'd recover a third time. He had to get away from her, from this, from their past, and the suddenly compelling lure of a future with the woman he'd sworn he'd always hate.

Alicia blinked away from the startlingly beautiful view of the ocean awash with the sun's morning light. At the sound of a glass door sliding open, her heart gave a now familiar lurch at the sight of Graciano. He was fully dressed, in a pair of dark trousers and a white button-up shirt with the sleeves pushed to his elbows, and something inside of her tipped totally off balance.

'I didn't realise you were out here.'

Her heart flip-flopped.

'I was just having a coffee.' She pushed a smile to her lips, telling herself she was imagining the coldness to his tone. 'Want to join me?'

His response was immediate: a swift shake of his head. Her heart dropped to her toes.

Graciano didn't leave, so that was something. But the longer he stood there without speaking, just frowning, the more she felt the ground beneath her shift.

Did he regret what had happened? Was he angry with her again? If so, what on earth for? She racked her memory for their conversation the night before, but couldn't find a single point over which they'd argued.

Her stomach knotted and she turned away, her eyes chasing the lines of the ocean instead.

'I have meetings in Barcelona today.'

He was leaving. Running away?

She pursed her lips. 'I see.'

'I'll be back for dinner.'

She angled her face towards him, pride demanding she keep her feelings concealed. She wouldn't let him see that she was hurt by that—that she was worried. 'You don't have to report your movements to me.' She softened the acidity of the words with a tight smile.

'I thought you might notice my absence,' he said after a pause, a small shrug shifting his shoulders. 'It's a courtesy.'

'Noted.' She tapped the papers beside her—notes she'd been making about his event. 'I have plenty to keep me busy, don't worry.'

'I'm not worried. I'm just letting you know that I'll be gone for the day.'

'And I'm saying, I don't care.' Hurt made her words more acerbic, the stinging tone designed to hide the way he'd upset her so easily. 'What happened last night doesn't change anything, Graciano. You didn't tell me the first time you went away for work. You don't have to tell me this time. It's fine.' Bitterness flooded her body as she spoke words she didn't feel, as she picked a fight she didn't want, and for no reason other than that she was disappointed—disappointed that he'd come out here frowning and cool, rather than wrapping her in his arms and kissing her, disappointed that he'd immediately delineated a line between the passion they'd indulged the night before and how he wanted things to be outside the bedroom.

Disappointed that she'd let herself hope, even

without realising she was doing it, for more—for something different in her life. For Graciano.

For a family.

The thought was so strong, so achingly searing, that she almost gasped. Had she really let herself fantasise about that? About the last ten years evaporating into thin air, and them becoming parents to their daughter, one happy family after all this time?

What a fool!

'Isabella has my contact information. If you should need anything, just call.'

She forced an over-bright smile to her face. 'I'm sure that won't be necessary.'

His eyes bore into hers for several long seconds and then he turned and left, without so much as a goodbye. And she was glad. Glad he'd left, because suddenly her eyes stung with tears and she desperately didn't want him to see them, to know he'd done that, to know how he could affect her.

A moment later, she heard the helicopter whir to life and expelled a soft, shaking sigh.

It was a blessing that Graciano was so busy. The takeover was in the final stages of negotiations, an occupation he generally relished, for it was at the end that the advantage was all his. By then, he understood his opponent—and he always regarded the company he was buying as the opposition—and he knew which buttons to push to achieve his aims.

He usually relished focusing with a laser-like intensity on the final meetings, but today he was distracted—not enough to negatively impact his work, but enough to drag him down to the level of being a mere mortal, so he was angry with himself as the day wore on, and his mind felt more scattered than he could remember it feeling.

Graciano closed the door gratefully after his meeting, and paced to the windows overlooking Barcelona. The unique city with its striking architecture always filled his heart with satisfaction. It was here that he'd come when he had nothing, here that he'd built a fortune. This was his home—his place in the world, his land of opportunities. It was here that he was king of his castle. But his eyes gravitated south, in the direction of the sea just beyond Valencia, and in his mind, he was approaching the island and Alicia was in the turret, waiting for him, watching for him—needing and wanting him.

He swore under his breath, dragging a hand through his hair. This was messier than he'd appreciated. Harder than he'd thought. She was taking him over on a cellular level and he had no idea how to stop it, but he knew that he must. He knew that he couldn't let her become his sun and moon ever again—no one could be trusted to wield that kind of power. The whole point of this exercise was to prove he was stronger than the power she wielded over him—that he'd changed, grown, beyond Alicia and the way she made him feel.

It was here, in the office, in the corporate world, that he was at his best. Here, life was simple. He could control everything. He didn't care what people thought of him. He didn't care what enemies he made. There was an objective measure for success—financial achievement—and it was the only benchmark he cared about.

Alicia's place in his life and mind had to be as tightly controlled as any other facet of his life. Determination fired inside of him, and without skipping a beat, he moved to his desk and lifted his phone from the cradle.

'Book me a dinner somewhere. And call Isabella to let her know I'll be in the city tonight, rather than returning to the island.'

He hung up, wondering why having made that firm decision didn't feel better—why the expected weight, instead of lifting from his shoulders, seemed to have thudded deep inside his gut.

Alicia stared, frowning, at the empty chair, the nerves that had been fraying all day now jolting through her.

He wasn't coming back tonight.

The message had been relayed by Isabella with a casual air. After all, the housekeeper could have no idea how much Alicia was looking forward to seeing Graciano, how she'd been building up to asking him why he'd been in such a strange mood that morning.

Isabella couldn't have known what kind of rejection there was in those simple words.

But Alicia did.

She felt it deep in her soul.

There was no more effective way of telling her he regretted what had happened between them than by showing her, and that was exactly what he was doing. Could he put any more distance between them than he already was?

She stabbed her fork into the piece of fish, lifting it to her mouth and forcing herself to chew when she was no longer hungry. She'd skipped lunch, though, and she knew she should eat, but every time she went through the motions of putting food in her mouth, it became harder and harder to swallow.

Sleeping together had been a mistake. She'd let herself believe things could be different for them, but that had been a fool's paradise. Even if Graciano were capable of change, even if she were able to put her heart on the line again, nothing would change the fact that she'd kept their daughter from him, that he'd made it impossible to tell him, and then she'd accepted that. They both had a right for far too much resentment. There could be no coming back from that. There was no hope here.

She had to tell him about Annie. Not because of what had happened between them, but because it was the right thing to do. Annie was his daughter. He needed to know.

But…was that selfish? He'd made it clear he didn't want children. His answers on that score were unequivocal. Telling him might feel right to her—it might even feel good—but what if he chose to have nothing to do with Annie? What if Annie's existence ruined his life in some way?

She groaned softly, dropping her head forward with the sheer weight of worry that was pounding her from either side. She had no idea what to do, but sitting here pining for him wasn't an option.

Que cada palo aguante su vela. Every mast has its own sail.

She was her own person, more so now than she'd been at sixteen, when she'd had to submit to the strings of her life being pulled without her say so. Now she could pull back.

And there was no way in hell she was going to stay on this island, as much a prisoner as the original occupant of this house, desperately waiting for the scattered attentions of a man who didn't, or couldn't, be everything she wanted.

She had to leave.

CHAPTER NINE

HE'D PUSHED HIMSELF to remain away most of the following day, too. He told himself the emotion coursing through him was that of satisfaction, that he was glad he'd been able to resist her, to continue with his normal life. He refused to acknowledge the powerful zipping in his veins, the almost superhuman strength bursting inside of him that was the result of knowing he'd see her again soon—that his abstinence would be rewarded. They could share a meal; he could watch her and listen to her and admire her, then draw her to his room and make love to her all night long, safe in the knowledge his willpower was stronger than his need for her. Control. It was everything.

His body hardened as the helicopter came down low over the island, exulting in the prospect of the night ahead.

Until he looked out of the window and saw Alicia standing in the middle of the path that approached the helipad, just as he'd stood when she'd arrived days earlier. There was nothing untoward about that. He might even have found it exciting, except for the suitcase at her side and the impenetrable mask of steel her features bore.

* * *

'Alicia.' He practically growled her name as he drew close, and every single treacherous cell in her body went into high alert at his nearness, heat spooling between her legs, breasts aching for his touch. She ground her teeth and kept her eyes focused on a point just beyond his shoulder, on the helicopter that would soon—she hoped—take her part of the way home.

'Graciano,' she responded in kind, but without a hint of warmth in her voice.

'Going somewhere?'

'Yes.' Now she forced her eyes to meet his and her stomach dropped to her toes. 'Home.' The word quivered a little. She swallowed, tamping down on her emotions as she'd had to do for so many years. 'I've got everything I need, including your assistant's information. We had a long chat today. I know exactly how to proceed. There's no reason for me to remain here.'

'Isn't there?' he asked, moving dangerously close, his voice silky. Her throat hurt. She stood her ground.

'No.'

Perhaps he wasn't expecting the resistance. His eyes widened for the briefest moment. Then a scowl settled on his brow.

'However, we had an arrangement. Five nights.'

Her spine tingled. 'Our arrangement's changed.'

'Not from where I'm standing.'

'You'd seriously want to keep me here against my will?'

'Is that what I would be doing?'

She swallowed hard, ignoring the swirling desire moving through her, the desire that would wreak havoc with her life if she allowed it—not to mention her self-respect. As if he could read her thoughts, he moved forward, closer, dangerously close so her pulse fired into high frequency and her heart twisted.

'Stay,' he murmured, bringing his lips to the base of her throat, kissing her slowly. God, how she wanted to listen to him. Her bones felt as though they were made of molten lava.

'I've told you what I want,' she said, trying to be firm. 'I'd like to leave now.'

'That doesn't suit me.'

She glared at him. 'Why not?'

'Because we had a deal.'

'Oh, for crying out loud. Is that the sum total of your argument? Because if so, it just underscores *why* I'm right to leave.'

His eyes skimmed hers and she knew she'd said too much. She'd shown how hurt she'd been when she'd intended to keep that pain wrapped up inside herself.

'You're angry that I went away.'

There was no sense fighting that. 'I'm angry
I let you use me. I'm angry I didn't see through
you. And yes, I'm angry that you went away, but
I suppose there was no point in staying. You got
what you wanted. So now, just let me go.'

He swore softly, then caught her at the elbow
and turned her away. 'I didn't use you, Alicia.
What happened between us was very mutual,
very satisfying. Do not rewrite it.'

'I'm not coming back to the house with you,'
she said, her voice rising, approaching hysteria. She'd already mentally torn herself from the
beautiful place. She couldn't go back. 'I want to
go home.'

'I'm not going to have this conversation here,'
he said, gesturing to the helicopter pilot and the
open air around them. 'Come inside and we'll
talk.'

'There's no point.' She wrenched her arm free.
'Nothing you can say will change my mind. I
want to go. I have to go.'

'Why?'

*Because I'm one more sensual night away
from falling in love with you and I can't allow
that to happen. Because we have a daughter and
I need to tell you about her but I can't work out
how or when, when I'm on your island and in
your bed. But I will when I have finally found
the courage and the words.* She almost shouted

her response, so awash was she with feelings. 'Isn't it obvious?'

'What did you expect me to say and do the next morning? How did you want me to act?'

Her insides were bruised; his questions hurt. 'Like a decent human being?' she muttered, before she could think through her reply.

His face blanched visibly and all too late she remembered her father throwing those words at him back then. But the charge was deserved now. He'd treated her like dirt.

'You wanted flowers? Perhaps a string quartet to play to you from beneath my window?'

'Don't speak to me like that,' she ground out. 'You started pushing me away the second you woke up. I don't care that you've been in Barcelona, that you had to work. It's the *way* you told me. The way you spoke to me. The way you stayed silent while you were gone. What we shared—'

But she was moving into dangerous territory now, as truths she hadn't even acknowledged to herself seemed to be thrusting forward, demanding to be spoken.

'Was sex. As inevitable now as it was back then. We both agreed to that.'

Tears filmed her eyes and she blinked furiously, trying to stem their progress. 'If that's so, why are you fighting me about leaving? Why would you want to keep me here?'

A muscle jerked in his jaw as her question exploded between them. 'I'm a man of my word,' he said finally. 'I presumed you would also have a personal code of honour. Having agreed to stay for five days—'

'That's a load of crap,' she contradicted forcefully. 'You know better than anyone that circumstances change. I'm not staying here after what happened with us. I can't. And I know you're too good a person to make me.' Her voice cracked; her heart splintered. 'So stop arguing and tell your damned pilot to take me to Valencia.'

He dragged a hand through his hair and she waited, her nerves stretching tight, waiting, hoping he'd have something to say that would unlock the pain in her heart, setting it free, high above them, flying out over the ocean and dispersing for good.

There'd been so much pain in her life, and much of it was linked to this man.

Bitterness washed through her, and panic, too, because nothing would be the same after this. The question of Annie could no longer sit in abeyance. Alicia had to work out how to proceed. She knew she couldn't continue to abide by the decisions she'd made as a scared, lonely sixteen-year-old. Everything was so complicated, and the weight of that complexity pressed down on her now, making breathing almost impossible.

'Why do you want me to stay?' she asked when he didn't speak, and she could feel the situation slipping away from her. 'And don't say it's because we had a deal. The deal was for me to organise your event and that's well underway.'

'I want you to stay for the same reason we slept together.'

She held her breath.

'There's unfinished business between us.'

'I think it's finished now.'

'Do you?' He lifted a single brow, mockery in his face. 'So you'll fly away and never think of me again?'

Her eyes dropped to the ground between them, everything shifting wildly out of focus. She'd thought of him every day for the last ten years. She knew that wouldn't change. 'We'll never finish this,' she said after a beat. 'From the moment my father reacted the way he did, from the moment he made those threats, he set our lives on courses that could never come back together. There's nothing to be gained by this.'

He moved closer again, so close she caught a hint of his masculine, spiced fragrance, and her pulse went into overdrive, desire lurching through her. 'I want you out of my head,' he said finally, the admission wrenched from him, and she closed her eyes on the welling of grief, because she understood how he felt. They were each a torment to the other.

'So much so you're willing to keep me here, even when I've asked to leave?' she whispered, knowing the answer, knowing she was moments away from his acceptance.

They were both trapped by the past, by another man's choices, but one of them had to be strong enough to break free. Staying here wasn't the answer. Alicia needed to get back to her real life; she needed space to breathe and think, neither of which she could do here, where Graciano filled every single one of her senses—even with his absence.

'No,' he said, finally, the word shattering inside of her. 'I want you to stay, but the choice is yours.' He took a step back, crossing his arms over his chest and looking at her dispassionately, no emotion visible in his handsome face. His extreme control only underscored her reasons for needing to leave.

He might think she was under his skin, but he didn't understand what it was to feel, to love, to need, with an all-consuming passion. He couldn't fathom the torture she'd experienced because of her feelings for this man. She'd triumphed over those feelings once—she'd been strong and resilient and had made a life for her-self—but being around him threatened that com-pletely.

'Staying isn't an option.' In the end, it was that simple.

Only then did a flicker of feeling seep into his features, a look in his eyes that she'd seen once before, the morning after they'd slept together, when her father had berated him and thrown him off his property. Betrayal.

She sucked in a breath and spun away from him, blinking rapidly as her attention landed on the helicopter.

'Come with me,' he commanded, striding past her, picking up her suitcase, then moving to the helicopter.

It was a done deal; she was leaving. She'd gotten what she wanted and didn't feel a hint of satisfaction in that. Disappointment jarred her with every step she took, but she knew this was the right course of action. It was as it had to be.

The helicopter was barely in the air before he knew he'd made a rare mistake. Graciano, who was no expert at reading people, at manoeuvring them to do his bidding, had erred. His own feel-ings had been coursing through him, making it impossible to understand hers, to know how to respond to them, how to give her what she wanted.

He planted his hands on his hips and watched, grim-faced, as the helicopter lifted up, wondering if she was looking down at him, wondering if she was regretting her decision, too.

He knew one thing for certain: this wasn't the end for them. After ten years, he'd had enough. He wanted closure, and watching her walk away from him wasn't how he'd achieve it. There would be a better way. He just needed time to consider that, and come up with a plan.

'You're home!' Annie pushed back her chair, a huge grin on her face as she zipped around the table and towards Alicia. Alicia could only stand there, stricken by the sight of her daughter, and all the similarities to Graciano she'd been able to blot out for the past nine years that were now forcing themselves to be acknowledged—similarities not only to Graciano, but to his family. Annie's family.

She bent down so she could wrap her arms around Annie, hugging her little body tight, tears filming her eyes as she nuzzled into the curve of her neck and her silky dark hair. She inhaled, eyes closed, and then blinked open, so her gaze landed across the room on Diane, who was watching with a small frown.

'You're early!' Annie remarked, moving to pull back, except Alicia held her tight, as though her life depended on it—as though she knew that the world they'd built, of being just the two of them, could no longer go on.

'I finished ahead of schedule,' she said unevenly. 'And I wanted to come home.'

'Yay! How was it?'

'Lovely,' she lied.

'Did you take a billion photos? Diane showed me the one of the beach, but that's all. Did you go shopping? What was it like?'

Alicia laughed softly. 'I was working. I didn't get many photos.'

'But you took some?'

She thought of the beautiful beach, the gardens, and nodded. 'I'll show you in the morning. It's late now.' The only flight she could get out of Valencia had been an evening one, and it had been held up on the tarmac.

'Diane let me stay up watching a movie.'

'She did, did she?' Alicia tried to relax into the normalcy of this, the domestic contentment of her normal life, but she knew she no longer belonged quite the same way. She was different. Everything had changed.

'And eating ice cream.'

'Dibber dobber,' Diane responded, moving closer with a wink.

'Well, it's bedtime now.' Alicia pressed another kiss to her daughter's forehead, then straightened, heart heavy with the weight of her responsibilities.

Once Annie had padded upstairs, Diane propped a hip against the door, her silvering hair shimmering in the soft lamplight. 'You're upset.'

It was a correct guess, but Alicia shook her head, pushing a bright smile to her face. Diane was one of the few people who knew all of Alicia's secrets. She'd been there from the beginning, when Alicia had come to hospital appointments on her own and Diane, the paediatrician on call, had taken a special interest in the teenage mother. She'd held Alicia's hand when she'd tried to speak to Graciano and had seen her heartbreak when he'd rejected her.

'Yes,' she said, pulling her lips to one side. 'But I probably deserve to be.'

'Pish, what happened?'

Alicia sighed softly, then began to talk, to explain everything to Diane, who listened with a sympathetic, loving expression, nodding from time to time.

'Do you still love him, darling?' Diane asked, after a beat.

Alicia startled. 'Love him? Of course not. How can I?'

'Because you have the biggest heart of anyone

I know. You've been single ever since him. And you look as though you've left a part of yourself behind in Spain.'

Alicia opened her mouth to deny it again, but found her mind too swamped. 'It doesn't matter how I feel. We've both made too many mistakes, Di. You must see that? What future can there be for us, after all that's come before?'

The following day, Graciano flicked through the document, scowling.

There was no denying: it was excellent. With very little input from Graciano, Alicia had somehow planned the perfect evening—for his non-existent event. It was a shame he wasn't planning to host any such party, as it would have been exceptional. The plans were comprehensive and professional, detailing guest transportation, staffing needs as well as accommodation, dietary requirements, menu suggestions, marquee placement and dance floor. She'd suggested two music options: a DJ for by the beach, and more of a lowkey acoustic band for the dinner. She'd arranged for fireworks, scheduled interviews with several high-profile magazines… Everything had been thought of.

He got to the bottom, then quit the document, returning to the email she'd sent, rereading it for the tenth time.

Graciano,

Please see attached event plan. I've gone through the details with your assistant, who's happy to run point on the night. You shouldn't need anything more from me.

Best wishes,

Alicia

It was not unlike any number of emails he received on a daily basis, and that in and of itself was a problem.

She wasn't just some colleague…someone he'd employed for a job. She was Alicia.

Unfinished business, indeed.

With a grim expression on his features, he hit Reply.

Alicia,

I have some questions. Can we meet to discuss?

Graciano hesitated before he remembered he didn't second-guess himself and hit Send.

The ball was in her court, but he already knew what she'd say. No one who took such obvious pride in their professional abilities would disappoint a client.

He leaned back and waited, every cell in his body stretching taut for no reason he could think of.

* * *

She swore as she read the email. It wasn't completely unexpected, but it sent a thousand feelings rioting through her. She knew she'd need to see him again, to finally tell him about Annie, but it still felt almost impossible.

I can speak now.

She waited, and sure enough, the reply came through within a minute.

No, in person. I'll send a car.

Her heart leaped into her throat.

Are you in London?

Yes. What's your address?

Everything began to tremble.

I can't come right away. I have an appointment at four p.m.

She had Annie's parent-teacher interview scheduled for that afternoon.
The response was immediate.

Tonight?

Everything shifted. She wanted to tell him no and she wanted to tell him 'Hell, yes.' But at the end of the day, this was just business, the last of her obligation to him. He'd paid five hundred thousand pounds for the privilege, after all.

I can give you an hour. Six o'clock?

What's your address?

She shook her head. She wasn't going to let him send a car. She couldn't live in a world where Graciano knew where her house was.

I'll come to you.

If you prefer.

He included an address in Knightsbridge at the bottom of the email and she pushed her phone away like it was poison, before reaching for it once more to see if Diane—her saviour—was available to help with Annie.

She was.

Seeing Graciano again, then, was only a matter of time. And this time, she couldn't squander the opportunity.

She had to tell him about Annie. She'd gone to the island knowing she must, but wanting to learn more about him first. While he'd always be a form of poison to her, he was also the father of her child.

Nothing else mattered.

Not their past, not their future, not her heart, her wishes, their desire. They shared a daughter, and working out how to deal with that reality had to be their sole focus. It would take every single bit of nerve she possessed, but Alicia could wait no longer. Tonight would be the night.

CHAPTER TEN

SHE'D PRESUMED THE address would be for an office, but the moment she approached the front of the building, she realised the error of her ways. This was residential, plain and simple. She double-checked the email, seeing that the address included an entry code. She keyed it in and waited as the glass doors swished to let her pass.

The foyer was stately and impressive, with shiny tiles and a double-height ceiling, the wall-to-wall windows showing a view straight through to Hyde Park. It was spectacular. She moved to the bank of lifts and waited for one to arrive, then moved inside, again consulting her phone for instructions. She pressed the button that corresponded with the floor number he'd given her, then stepped back and waited. It whooshed up quickly, leaving her tummy back in the foyer.

When the doors opened, it was into a small room, with a leather bench seat and an impressively ornate mirror. She caught a glimpse of herself, pale and nervous, and pinched her cheeks, sucking in a deep breath before pressing the doorbell for the only door in the place.

Her nerves stretched tight and she discreetly

observed the time—just before six. Maybe he wasn't home? Maybe he'd forgotten? Her heart trembled and she tried to work out how she felt about either possibility, and then, the door pulled inwards.

Graciano stood on the other side, and all she could do was stare, as Diane's question went round and round in her head. *Do you love him?*

She'd denied it to Diane, and to herself, but now, she had to face reality: yes, she loved him. Still. As much as ever. She'd never stopped.

'Alicia.' Apparently oblivious to her emotion turmoil, he stepped back and waved an arm into the apartment. She hesitated on the threshold, aware that crossing it was a metaphorical hurdle as well as a physical one.

'I don't bite,' he growled, so she startled, moving past him quickly and putting as much distance between them as she could, but his eyes held hers for several beats and then dropped lower, his appraisal swift but fiercely hot, burning her with the intensity of his scrutiny. His gaze scraped hungrily over her frame, over the business suit and two-inch spike heels she wore—a confidence boost, usually. She trembled and turned away from him a little.

Had it really only been ten days since they'd seen each other? It felt like so much longer, and

at the same time, it felt like no time had passed
at all.

The reality of their situation, of all she had to
tell him, burst and suddenly her stomach was in
knots. This was terrifying.

'Thank you for coming,' he responded, gesturing deeper into the apartment before taking
some steps towards the spectacular windows
framing a view of the busy street and Harrods
just down a little way.

She lifted her shoulders. 'I'm a professional.'

'So I gather. I was impressed by your proposal.'

Her heart fired. 'But you have questions?'

'I'll come to that. Would you like a drink?'
He moved to the back wall, into a large, open-
plan kitchen that would have been at home in a
five-star restaurant.

She shook her head. 'I'd prefer to get this over
with.'

His eyes hummed across her face. 'Still ada-
mant you don't want anything to do with me?'

Her nerves jumbled faster. 'I'm not here to
discuss what happened between us.'

'Why not?'

'For all the reasons we discussed on the island.
Primarily—' she sighed '—there's no point.'

'I disagree.'

She hesitated, then moved closer to the kitchen,

staying on the opposite side of the bench, glad
for the physical barrier between them.

'I made a mistake.'

She watched as he pulled a bottle of sparkling
water from the fridge, then poured two glasses.
Alicia pretended fascination with the bubbles.

'Oh?'

'I didn't handle things well.'

Her heart slammed into her ribs. 'I don't want
to talk about events of a decade ago.'

He frowned reflexively. 'I mean last week.
When I went to Barcelona, the day after we slept
together, I was running, but it was insensitive
and hurtful. I'm sorry.'

It was the very last thing she'd expected. Her
lips parted on a soft exhalation and the knots
in her tummy grew bigger. 'Graciano,' she said
after a beat, looking down at the countertop.

'Let me say this,' he asked urgently, leaning
across and putting a hand on hers.

She swallowed past a knot in her throat, then
nodded once.

He came around to her side of the bench, moving so close to her that her treacherous body
trembled in immediate response.

'Twice in my life I have been without an anchor—the first time, when my parents died and
my brother disappeared.' She dug her nails into

her palms, knowing what was coming. 'And the second time was when I left you.'

Her heart twisted.

'I was almost destroyed, twice.'

She closed her eyes, the emotions too, too real.

'I refuse to let it happen a third time.'

Her heart broke for him, then, and it broke for her, too. Her father had destroyed so much, but they'd been complicit. He'd been complicit by letting that rejection destroy him instead of fighting for what he must have known was the truth.

'You were wrong to leave,' she said after a beat.

'You think I should have let the police throw me in prison?'

'I would have defended you.'

'You see everything through your eyes, through your privilege. I was a street kid. There was no one who'd believe me over your father. Besides, you couldn't even defend me to him.'

Sadness welled inside of her.

'Why not tell me that?' she asked quietly. 'Why not tell me that you'd left for self-pres-ervation?'

'I was too angry,' he said with a shift of his shoulders.

'We're going in circles here,' she said throatily. 'And I'm not convinced any of it matters any-

more.' Sadness engulfed her. She loved him, and
she'd have put money on him having loved her
at one time, but that didn't mean they'd be able
to make it work.

'It matters,' he responded gruffly, closing the
distance between them, putting his hands on her
hips to hold her steady. 'I knew I'd made a mistake as soon as your helicopter left. I want more
time with you.'

It should have delighted her, but she heard the
restrictions in his statement. 'How much time?'

He lifted his shoulders. 'More.'

'Until you're over me?' She pushed, merci-
lessly, because she needed his absolute honesty.
This wasn't love. It wasn't everlasting, for all
eternity, happily-ever-after love. His offer was
limited, driven by sex and ego.

'Until we're *both* ready to move on,' he corrected carefully. 'Tell me you don't want that.'

'God,' she laughed unevenly, sadly. 'What I
want? You have no idea of the gulf that exists
between what I want and what I can have. You
have no bloody idea.'

'Then tell me,' he demanded, moving closer
so their bodies were touching and his lips were
an inch from hers. 'Show me.'

And he kissed her, a slow, searching kiss that
curled her toes and made everything shimmer
like gold dust.

'Does anything matter when there's this?'

She was on the edge of a cliff, her feet nudging farther and farther into open air, a fall imminent. She clung to him—her saviour and danger. He stared down at her, his eyes inscrutable, desire zipping through her, other feelings, more dangerous, more cloying, tightening around her. But in the back of her mind there was Annie and the past, her father, their lost opportunities and the reality she had to face: they hadn't loved each other enough to make this work. If that had been the case back then, it would definitely condemn their relationship now.

'This can't happen,' she mumbled, but even as she said it, she was lifting up, seeking his lips, knowing it was impossible but wanting him anyway. 'I can't—'

'Don't overthink it,' he said into her mouth and she bit back a sob, knowing there was wisdom in that—or was it self-interest? She wanted him enough to almost mute all sense and logic. But not quite.

'I need to talk to you.'

'About the event? Later.'

'No, not that. I need—'

He pulled back, pressing a finger to her lips. 'Later.' The word was laced with the same fierce need burning her alive. Defiance, though, had her staying where she was, separated from him by an inch.

'Are you sure you're not going to disappear into thin air again?'

His response was to kiss her, slowly at first, then with the need that was building inside of them so their bodies were moving deeper into the penthouse, away from the kitchen, to the plush leather sofas and back onto them, a tangle of limbs and clothes as they discarded them, shucking desperately, needing nakedness and to be together.

She held her breath as he paused to sheathe himself and then drove into her, the relief immediate and complete, so she barely heard the low rumbling of her phone. All she was conscious of was Graciano, his movements, his body, so powerful and strong, and she tilted her head back, sweat beading her forehead as she bit down on her lip and surrendered to this completely, knowing then that she could never have enough of him, knowing that she would go anywhere and do anything to be with him, for the chance to be like this.

It was a terrifying realisation and even more so because she could no longer deny what fuelled her—the love that ran though her. It was a love she'd felt the moment they'd met, a love that had grown as they'd spent time together, that had exploded the night they'd made love, and that she'd clung to all these years, an oasis in the midst of the desert of difficulties that had been her life for so long.

Tears filled her eyes as an orgasm built inside of her and then she was tilting over the edge, nails scoring marks down his back, and he was right there with her, his voice rising, his hands holding her hips steady, his face over hers clenched, his eyes squeezed shut. She stared at him as she tipped over the edge, fascinated, overwhelmed and so full of love that she almost couldn't bear it.

She was conscious of their bodies all tangled together, their loud breathing, his breath warm against her forehead, the feeling that they'd burst an oversized balloon, the sense of relief even as his proximity was stirring new feelings to life— and then, finally, she was conscious of a buzzing noise, faraway seeming at first and then, not so far away. Just across the room.

'Your phone?' he asked, pushing up onto his palms and looking down at her.

She almost wanted to tell him it didn't matter. It was hard to muster any interest in the outside world, but maternal instincts weren't easy to switch off, and despite the fact Annie was with Diane, a premonition of disaster that was always easy to reach for had Alicia putting a hand on Graciano's chest.

'I'd better check it.'

He cocked a brow but moved to release her, pulling out of her body so she bit back a groan of complaint, and he stood, pacing across the room to retrieve her handbag. He carried it to Alicia, allowing her to marvel at his frame, his masculinity, his strength and power.

'Thank you,' she murmured, a smile whispering at the corners of her lips. She lifted her phone from her bag and saw Di's name, and a hint of guilt coloured her cheeks pink. Somehow, she'd still managed to fail at telling Graciano about his daughter! 'I have to take this.'

And then the truth, she promised herself, swiping the phone to answer.

'Hi, Di.'

Graciano turned and strode to the kitchen, then pulled out a beer and popped the top off it.

'Don't panic.'

'Oh, God.' Her heart sunk and she was standing, looking around for her underwear. Graciano had frozen in response to the tone, beer midway to lips, and now he replaced it on the counter. 'What's happened?'

'I said don't panic.'

'"Don't panic" is what people say when

there's something to panic about. Is it Annie? Di? What's happened?'

She stretched her knickers on, then her trousers, breath rushed.

'She's okay, but we're on our way to hospital.'

'Hospital? Oh, my God. Why? Where? Which hospital?'

She named one in Hammersmith, just across the Thames from her flat. She knew Diane consulted from there sometimes. 'There was an accident at football training.'

Alicia squeezed her eyes shut. 'Please stop being so vague and tell me exactly what's happened. I can handle it.'

Guilt was a dagger in her stomach. She kept the phone pressed to her ear as she hooked her bra into place. Out of the corner of her eye, she saw Graciano matching her, dressing, without the sense of panic but with all the efficiency.

'She collided with another player and got knocked into the goal. Her arm is broken.'

Alicia swore, all the colour draining from her face. 'Is she in pain?'

'Yes, darling, she is.'

It was so like Di—a doctor—not to sugarcoat it.

'But she'll live. She needs to get it set and at this time of night, a hospital's the best place.' Di paused. 'While I'm there, I want to get her head checked out. She hit it pretty hard as well.'

Alicia's stomach was in knots. 'I'm coming right away. I can be in Hammersmith within fifteen, twenty minutes at the most.' She cursed the fact it was peak hour, that the roads between Knightsbridge and Hammersmith would be at their busiest.

'Tell her Mummy's coming. Tell her I love her.'

'She's going to be okay. This is just a precaution. You don't mess around with head injuries is all. Try not to worry.'

'Just tell her, okay?'

She disconnected the call, turning to Graciano without really seeing him. 'I have to go.' This was a God-awful mess, but her situation with the Spaniard had been bumped lower on her priority list—so, too, the conversation she knew they had to have. This wasn't the time.

'To Hammersmith, I heard. I'll drive you.'

It should have raised alarm bells—she should have known to fight it—but in that moment, anything or anyone who could make this journey easier earned her gratitude.

'Come on. My car's downstairs.'

She was strangely calm as they rode the elevator in silence, but once she was in Graciano's black four-wheel drive with the engine throbbing beneath her, an overwhelm of hysteria bubbled inside of her so she had to look out of the window to muffle her soft sob.

For several minutes neither spoke, but then, as they crossed through South Kensington, he pulled up at the lights and turned to face her.

'You have a child.'

It was like the dropping of a blade, right against the side of her neck.

She swallowed hard and nodded, eyes stinging. 'Annie.' She whispered their daughter's name.

'Why didn't you tell me?' His features showed surprise, shock that she'd kept this from him.

She groaned, pressing her head back against the headrest. 'It just…wasn't that simple.'

'Why not? It seems like a very easy sentence to form. "I have a daughter."'

It wasn't how she'd wanted to tell him, but there was no way she could carry on without being honest. 'Annie's nine,' Alicia said, the words trembling in the car.

The light turned green and Graciano took off, but his knuckles were white against the wheel as her revelation sunk in. Silence met that statement, but it was a silence that was heavy with the turning of his brain as he analysed that from all angles.

South Kensington morphed into Earl's Court

and then West Ken, all more familiar to Alicia now.

'Nine,' he said, pulling up at another set of lights, turning to face her. 'So you had her soon after we were together.'

Alicia nodded, her throat thick. 'About eight months later, actually.'

His eyes flared wide and she could see the genuine surprise in his features. This was the last thing he'd been expecting. Her knees trembled.

'I wanted to tell you.'

He swore, then accelerated as the lights changed, his gaze focused straight ahead.

'I came over tonight to tell you—'

'That I have a daughter?' he roared, gripping the steering wheel again, an obvious attempt to regain control. 'She is *nine*,' he said, the words dragged from him. 'And this is the first I am hearing of her?'

Alicia squeezed her eyes shut. 'I tried to tell you.'

'When? When did you goddamned try to tell me about my daughter? She is *nine*,' he repeated, in shock.

His anger was understandable—she'd expected it—but that didn't mean it hurt any less.

'I tried to tell you,' she said again, sucking

in a deep breath. 'Back then, when I found out. You made it impossible.'

He snorted. 'Come on, how can that be?'

'You told me you didn't want to hear from me—'

'So you blurt out that you're pregnant!' he roared. 'You *find a way*.'

She shook her head. 'You think that's easy? I was sixteen, completely alone, living in a foreign country, terrified, hurt, rejected and ashamed.' She twisted her face away from him. 'You were awful when I *did* call.'

'So your pride was hurt, and therefore you kept my child from me?'

'You don't even want children!' she snapped.

'Don't.' His lips pressed together, and she knew that was a mistake. How he felt about a hypothetical child was completely different to how he might feel about a daughter already in the world.

'Fine.' She lifted a hand appealingly. 'But you have to see this my way—'

'No,' he refuted swiftly, driving through Hammersmith without so much as a glance at Alicia. 'I don't. I need only see the facts.' He pulled up on a double yellow line outside the hospital. 'You have had nine years to tell me about her—'

'You're not exactly an easy person to speak

to!' she said quickly. 'After you changed your number, I had literally no way to find you.'

'Through my office?'

'I tried. But short of telling the receptionist who answered our personal business—'

'Why not do that?' he demanded fiercely. 'Why not do whatever it took to get this information to me? Do you think I would *ever* have chosen to be absent from her life if I'd known?'

A huge lump formed in Alicia's throat. 'I don't know,' she said with a shake of her head. 'I just know that I wanted to tell you, and then I rationalised that it was better this way.'

He swore in Spanish. 'That's convenient for you.'

'Don't,' she spat, putting her hand on the car door. 'Don't you dare imply that I took the easy way out. If you had *any* idea how hard this has been for me, how much I struggled raising our daughter on my own…'

'Because of a choice you made,' he said, unrelenting. Her heart hurt. She loved him, but she hated him, and she could see more clearly than ever that any future was impossible for them. There was too much water under the bridge, far too much resentment.

He opened his car door, stepping out into the evening, hands on hips. She did the same, staring at him over the bonnet of the car.

'Graciano, I'm—'

'Which way?' he interrupted, eyes boring into hers.

She blinked away, staring up at the hospital, then sucking in a deep breath. 'You can't mean to come in with me?'

'She's my daughter, too, isn't she?'

Alicia bit into her lip. 'Yes, but this isn't the time to meet her. This is a little girl we're talking about, and she deserves better than to have this kind of drama. Especially when she's hurting. Just—go home. I'll call you when I know what's happening.'

'This is my daughter.' He ground the words out.

'I know.' She shivered, but not from the cool evening air. 'I get that. But this isn't about us right now.'

'No, it's about her. It's about the fact she has a father she knows—*Cristo,* I have no idea what you've told her about me.'

Tears welled in Alicia's eyes as she stalked towards him, needing him to understand.

'She's my family,' he said firmly, and her heart squished, because she understood, better than anyone, what that meant to him. He'd been robbed of his family already, and now Alicia had done the same thing. Guilt was an unavoidable wave, crashing over her.

'I must see her.'

'I… I'm worried it will upset her.'

'You think I can't control myself?' His nostrils flared angrily.

She knew the opposite was likely true, but that didn't change a thing.

'I can't…stand here and argue with you. I need to go to her.' She lifted a hand to his chest but he flinched, pulling away from her. 'Just, please,' she whispered. 'Don't do anything to upset her. She has to be our priority.'

The look of anger in his eyes turned her heart to ice, but she couldn't stay there and dwell, nor could she try to fix this. Annie needed her.

She checked her phone as she swept into the hospital, approaching the triage nurse's desk.

'My daughter's here, with Dr Wallace.'

'Ah, yes. They've just gone up to orthopaedics. Third floor, turn left at the elevators.'

'Thank you.' She didn't wait for Graciano but knew he was right there with her, and even though she'd fought this, even though she could feel his fury, she was glad he was there. There was strength in his presence, and she needed that strength in that moment, more than ever.

'Di?' A tear slid down her cheek at the familiar sight of her dearest friend. Alicia sped up, mov-

ng down the corridor to where Di was waiting,
glasses around her neck, clipboard in hand.

'There you are, darling,' Di reached in for a
hug, eyes flicking to the handsome stranger in
Alicia's wake. 'Now, there's nothing to worry
about.'

'Her arm's not broken?' Alicia pulled away to
look in Di's face.

'Oh, it sure is, in two places. She did a real
good job of it.' Di tsked. 'Then again, that's our
Annie. Doesn't do anything by halves.'

'Can I see her?'

'Sure. She's just with Dr Wallace, but you can
go in.'

Diane's gaze lingered on Graciano, but Alicia
couldn't worry about anything besides Annie.
She slipped into the hospital room, pushing
past all of her tangled emotions to offer Annie
a smile.

He was moving slowly, dread and disbelief half
paralysing his limbs, but eventually, short of
stopping completely, it was no longer possible
to push this moment back, even for a second.

He stepped to the open door and hovered on
the edge of it, eyes flicking into the room, ignoring the silver haired woman who'd just been
locked in conversation with Alicia.

A young girl sat propped in bed, head bent

forward so her dark, silky hair formed a curtain around her features. Music was playing from a nearby iPhone. She wore a shiny blue-and-yellow football shirt and her nails were painted fluorescent green. When she moved slightly, he saw that her cheek was bruised, and then she lifted her head, looking around the room idly, as if bored, until her eyes landed on him.

It was like being punched, hard, in the solar plexus.

This was his daughter.

Fierce, out-of-control paternal pride burst to life. She was a part of him, a part of his brother and mother and father—a part of his family, unmistakably. She was a dead ringer for his mother, except her eyes, which reminded Graciano of his brother. Her skin was brown like his, but then she smiled a little curiously and he saw Alicia, and felt his heart buckle. Every idea of not wanting children burst into flames at the sight of this little person who was, unmistakably, of him.

'Hi.'

He couldn't look at Alicia, standing beside the bed. Anger was rushing through him, a tsunami of blame and recrimination meaning he wanted to exclude her from this moment. This was about Graciano and his daughter, about the connection he deserved to have felt from this child's birth—not now, nine years later.

'Hello.' He knew enough to fill the silence, to take control of the conversation.

The doctor flicked her gaze up, then returned to her work of setting the cast.

'It looks as though you've done an excellent job on that.' He nodded towards her arm.

'Broken in two places.' Annie nodded. His heart lurched. She was so utterly familiar to him—it was like discovering a piece of him he hadn't even realised was missing. 'Have you ever broken a bone?'

'My nose.' He pointed to the bump halfway down. 'And my wrist.'

She pulled her lips to the side in a gesture that was pure Alicia. It was like being stabbed.

'Are you family?' the doctor asked, her tone casual, he imagined, to a child, but Graciano heard the undertone. She was sounding him out.

'He's with me.' Alicia's voice was weak and watery, but it was enough. Rather than hold back and stay silent, she was speaking up now, not like ten years earlier. But it was hardly a ringing endorsement of her courage: she was speaking to keep him secret from Annie. That was all.

'And you are?'

'That's my mum,' Annie said, conspiratorially. 'Don't worry, I'm okay,' Annie reassured her, a lopsided smile on her lips.

He felt excluded. He felt lost. He felt fascinated by this daughter of his, by this beautiful, interesting girl he knew nothing about.

'Oh, darling.' He watched as Alicia quickly stepped to the edge of the bed and pressed a kiss to Annie's forehead. 'What happened?'

'It was just a collision, Mum.'

Alicia frowned, obviously not convinced.

'How do you know my mum?' She returned her attention back to Graciano, apparently far more interested in him than debriefing a football accident.

Alicia spoke first again, desperate to conceal the truth. It was the right thing to do, but in that moment, all he could see was her cowardice and shame, the lies she'd been telling for ten years that tripped off her tongue without premeditation now.

'I was doing some work for Graciano,' she said.

'In Spain?'

He interrupted before Alicia could answer. 'Yes, that's right. Have you ever been to Spain, Annie?'

'No, but I'm learning the language.'

Something shifted in his chest. 'Are you?'

'Mummy's teaching me.'

'She's very good.'

His eyes slashed through Alicia. Was that any wonder? The girl was half Spanish. The language, like many other hallmarks of his culture, ran through her veins. He noted the way Alicia wouldn't meet his eyes a second before he noticed the red rash across the base of her jaw, caused by his stubble. It was a confusing reminder, a white flag of surrender in the midst of his anger.

He ignored it.

'Do you like football, Annie?'

'It's one of my favourite things.'

'Are you any good?'

She laughed. 'I don't know. I like it a lot.'

'Annie's very—'

He threw Alicia a fulminating glare and she fell silent. He felt like a jackass, even when *he* was the one who'd been lied to.

'Okay.' The doctor snapped her rubber gloves off and stood, smiling. 'You're all done. Mind if I speak to you outside?' She addressed the question to Alicia, who hesitated a moment.

He ground his teeth together. Would she really not leave him alone with their daughter for even a few minutes? Dutifully, to avoid the same scene Alicia wanted to avoid, he moved through the door before she did, standing a little way down the corridor with his feet planted and arms crossed.

He watched as the doctor spoke to Alicia, the delineation between them clear. Legally, he wasn't her parent. He had no claim here, no business pushing into the conversation or demanding to know what was going on, but hell, morally, he did. That was his child. His family. All his life, he'd known that blood was thicker than water, yet Alicia had deprived him of Annie.

'She seems okay to me. Di wants her held overnight, for observation, and I'm happy to do that. It's sensible after a hit like she had, but so far, all the signs are good. She certainly didn't have any trouble remembering song lyrics, and could sing without slurring. Her focus is good and her eyes followed me as I spoke. Can you sit with her for a while longer?'

'I'll stay all night.'

The doctor smiled. 'There's a call button on the side of the bed. Just press it if you need anything.'

'What about her arm?'

'I'll put some notes in with her discharge file. She'll have to wear the cast for ten days, then get another X-ray to see how it's healing. Hopefully she can have it off at that point, but otherwise, she might need it to be set for another month or so.'

'She'll hate that,' Alicia remarked wryly, looking beyond the doctor to Graciano, then wishing she hadn't when the bottom fell out of her world again. 'Thank you for everything.'

'It's no problem. I'm here until three. I'll come by and see you again soon.'

'Thank you.'

What else was there to say?

She cast a glance over her shoulder into Annie's room; she was playing Tetris one-handed on Di's phone. Alicia took a step away from her daughter's—their daughter's—room, towards Graciano. His face was a sheer thundercloud.

'That's my daughter,' he said, so quietly she barely heard. But she understood. Learning you have a child is one thing—seeing them was quite another, and particularly when they looked as Annie did. She was the spitting image of him, and his family.

'Yes,' she whispered. 'I'm sorry—'

'For God's sake, no more apologies.' His nostrils flared. 'They are useless. I'm not interested in having you say sorry.'

She flinched. His voice was low, and yet the words cut deep.

'Then what are you interested in?'

'The next step.'

Her heart skipped a beat.

'Meaning?'

'Meaning, right now, I want to go in there and take my child away from this goddamned place, away from you, to raise her with me.' He glared at Alicia, who couldn't conceal her terror at that suggestion, but he didn't—couldn't—stop. 'I want to hire the best damned lawyers in the country and sue for full custody. I want to get judicial approval to move her to Spain. I want to make you feel what I'm feeling now, to know you have a child who you've missed out on so much of their life.'

She startled at his vehemence, pressing her back against the wall.

'That's not fair,' she whispered.

'Do not speak to me of *fair*.'

She lifted a shaking hand to her forehead, pressing it there as she stared up at him. An hour ago, they'd been making passionate, senseless love; now it was quite clear that he hated her.

'Write your address and phone number into my phone.' He handed it to her, then turned his back, breathing hard.

She did as he'd asked—there was no point keeping her details from him now. He knew about Annie. The game was up, not that it was ever anything like a game.

'I cannot believe you kept this from me,' he muttered, taking the phone and slamming it into his pocket. She was too shocked to refute that, to remind him she'd tried to tell him. 'I'll call you tomorrow to arrange a time to discuss this.

And I'll expect you to keep me informed of her progress here.'

'Okay.' She couldn't think straight, but she knew his request was hardly unreasonable. She opened her mouth to say something—though what, she wasn't sure—but he spoke first.

'I will never forgive you for this.'

He left, and she felt as though the light in her life had been switched off completely.

CHAPTER ELEVEN

ALICIA WAS AT serious risk of pacing a hole in the carpet, but she couldn't stop moving. As the minutes ticked by and the time of Graciano's arrival drew closer, her body simply wouldn't stay still. She was like a live wire, incapable of anything but jerking and shifting.

She flicked another glance at her watch, groaning audibly to see how slowly time was moving. Anxiety was running through her. She'd been waiting for the executioner's blade to drop ever since the hospital two nights earlier, and now, Sunday afternoon, with Annie and a school friend seeing a movie together, she had this small window of time in which she could try to make some order from the wreckage of her life.

Of course, that depended entirely on Graciano, and how reasonable he was prepared to be. It depended on if he'd even give her a chance to explain.

But she sucked in a breath and reminded herself of her new favourite expression: *Que cada palo aguante su vela.*

He might be angry with her, and rightfully so, but that didn't change the facts. It didn't mean she'd been wrong, only that he didn't understand yet. It was her job to make him see things from her perspective. He might continue to feel furious with her, for what he'd lost. That would be his right. But at least if she'd told him the full story, she'd know she'd done the best she could.

The doorbell rang and she moved to it, knowing that her future depended on the next thirty or so minutes of her life.

Anxiety was a raging fire in her belly as she unlocked it and drew the door inwards, her nerves flaming at the sight of Graciano. Today he was all that was dark, dangerous and sinfully delicious, from his black jeans and dark grey T-shirt to the expression he bore—a scowl crossed with a look of white-hot accusation.

None of it helped her nerves.

'Hi,' she murmured under her breath, then cleared her throat. 'Come in.'

He stepped into the hall behind her, his eyes scanning the walls as he took in the mishmash of photos—Alicia and Annie, photos of the many moments that made up their day-to-day life.

His scowl deepened.

'I've made a pot of coffee. It's not quite as fancy as your espresso, of course.' She was nervous—over-talking. She grimaced and moved into the living room, a happy space that caught the afternoon sun and invited one to sit down and settle in. She gestured to the sofas, covered in bright cushions and blankets, and moved to the tray on the coffee table.

'Can I get you a cup?'

He put his hands on his hips, his nostrils flaring as he expelled a slow breath, then dipped his head once. Glad for something to do, she poured a cup from the French press, then moved towards him, holding it out. His eyes seared hers for a moment before he took it, their fingers brushing so her stomach catapulted through her body.

'I want to explain—'

Breath hissed from between his teeth, so she faltered.

'It's important,' she finished softly.

He took a drink from the coffee cup, then moved away from her to place it on a side table. He crossed his arms, feet planted wide apart—hardly a gesture of welcome invitation, but she had to get through this.

'When I found out I was pregnant—'

'How did you find out?' he interrupted, but dispassionately, as though it were a fact-finding mission.

'I did a test.'

'Why?'

She frowned, remembering that weekend. 'It was in the middle of a bracing heat spell. I'd gone down to the lake to swim, and as I floated on my back, I just realised that my cycle was late—that I'd been swimming almost every day since you left.' She didn't add that it was one of the mechanisms she'd used to cope, that swimming reminded her of him, of being immersed in Graciano in the same way the water wrapped around her. 'I wasn't well informed,' she said wryly. 'But I'd watched enough TV shows to know that your period being late generally meant one thing.'

'So what did you do?'

'I skipped school one day,' she said, plunging herself back into the past. 'And went to a free clinic. I used a fake name, because my dad seemed to know everyone and I was terrified of him finding out.' She toyed with the necklace she wore. 'They gave me a pregnancy test and told me to come back if it was positive. They also gave me a handful of condoms,' she added with a tight smile, an attempt to lighten the mood, but Graciano's face was like a storm cloud.

'The test was positive,' she said with a lift of her shoulders.

'And then?' His eyes were locked to her face, holding her still. She stared at him, but she was sixteen again, uncertain, terrified and also giddy with excitement at the life growing inside of her.

'I didn't know what to do,' she admitted. 'My father was barely speaking to me and I had no other family except his mother, whom I hadn't seen in years. I hadn't been allowed to see friends since you left, to speak to anyone. I was living in a prison.'

His eyes narrowed for the briefest flash of time before his face resumed a mask of unbreakable control.

He didn't speak. She moved to the coffee, pouring herself a cup even though she wasn't sure her nerves needed any extra ammunition.

'There was no one I could turn to. No one who could help me make sense of any of it.' She lifted a hand to her hair, tucking it behind her ear. His eyes followed the gesture and her stomach kicked, a confusing array of feelings rioting through her slim frame.

'The first time I called you was a brutal experience,' she whispered, turning her back on him, then moving towards a picture of Annie that hung across the room. It had been taken just before her fourth birthday. Alicia still saw this smiling face in her mind when she closed her eyes. 'I was so in love with you.' She shook her head slowly.

'That wasn't love,' he responded acerbically. 'It was teenage hormones.'

The pain she felt was as real as if she'd been stabbed in the belly.

'For me, it was love,' she said. There was no

point in denying it, but nor did she need to wax lyrical about all the ways in which Graciano had brought her soul to life. 'I missed you like I'd lost a limb.'

She kept her back to him so didn't see his expression, didn't see the way he closed his eyes and inhaled.

'I didn't come here to talk about us. I want to know about my daughter.'

'Aren't the two inseparable?' she wondered aloud, her throat dry and sore, then pushed on, ignoring his interjections. There was a story to tell, and she couldn't skip ahead, but she could truncate it. 'I was devastated by what had happened between us, traumatised by the way my father had been. I didn't know you'd gone so far away. I called, the first time, because I wanted to come to you. I wanted to run away and be with you.' She lifted a hand to her heart, pressing it there in an attempt to stop the twisting pain. 'But your feelings had changed.' A divot formed between her brows as she recalled his repeated insistence that it had just been sex, not love. 'Or maybe they hadn't. Maybe I'd mistaken your feelings all along. That would make sense, given how easy you found it to shut me down.'

She sipped her coffee, eyes on Annie's face in the picture, not seeing the pallor of Graciano's.

'So when I found out I was pregnant, I was

scared to tell you. Even you. I was totally alone, Graciano. No family, no friends, and no you.'

Silence, while she brought herself together, and she waited for him to speak. Eventually, he did.

'I used a condom.'

Her eyes swept shut. He was determinedly focused on Annie's conception. Nothing more. The difficulties Alicia had faced meant nothing to him. *Because he doesn't love you.* Realising that she loved Graciano changed nothing about his feelings.

'Regardless of the fact you'd made your feelings clear to me, you were still the one person I thought I could turn to. This was *our* baby,' she said bitterly. 'And in spite of what you'd said on the phone that afternoon, I knew you'd help me.'

He didn't speak, but now sadness and hurt were turning to anger.

'Do you remember that call?'

His eyes bore into hers and then he nodded, once. 'I was angry.'

'Yes. You were. My world was falling apart and I turned to you, needing you, needing help—' She left the words suspended in mid-air. 'I wanted to tell you, Graciano. I never intended to do this on my own.'

'So why didn't you?'

'Come on. How? How could I?' She moved

o him instinctively, needing him to understand. 'I was still in love with you, heartbroken over what had happened, and you told me none of it meant anything to you. You told me to stop calling you—that you never wanted to hear from me again. You were awful.'

'Yes,' he said after a beat. 'I was.' He shoved a hand in his pocket, his eyes moving to the picture of Annie. 'But you were pregnant. No matter what I said, you should have found a way to tell me.'

'In theory, sure, but I was a scared, rejected sixteen-year-old. It's very easy to say that now, to see with clarity how I should have behaved, but back then, I was completely shut down by that call. I was destroyed.'

His mask slipped for just a moment, and she saw the anguish on his features. She wanted to weep for how their lives had unravelled.

'So what did you do next?'

'What could I do? I told my father.' She winced. 'It didn't go down well.'

Graciano's lips compressed, forming a tight, white line in his face.

'He called me every name under the sun, then slapped me.' She lifted a hand to her cheek, remembering the sting of that assault, aware of the way Graciano's bigger body startled now at the admission. 'Within an hour, he'd dropped me at the airport. We haven't seen each other since.'

'Bastardo.'

'Yes. Apparently I made a mockery of all his teachings.'

'He made a mockery of his teachings,' Graciano corrected.

'I came to live with my grandmother. She was...helpful,' Alicia said with a frown. 'Not loving, not even kind, really, but she did enable me to go back to school, and she helped with Annie when she was little.'

'Did you try to contact me at any other point?' he asked, again, focusing solely on the matter of Annie.

She bit down on her lower lip. 'I have thought about it every day.'

His eyes bore into hers and she felt as though so much was riding on her next few statements. 'When Annie took her first steps, I tried to contact you. I was overwhelmed with a need for you to know.' She shook her head slowly. 'Do you have any idea how hard you are to contact?'

He closed his eyes for a moment; his face was impossible to read.

'I tried,' she said softly. 'But I gave up quickly.' Only the truth would do. 'I was still just a kid.'

'Yes.' It was an admission she hadn't expected. 'And since then?'

She lifted her fingers and ran them over the ends of her hair. 'You've become even harder to contact,' she said frankly. 'Your success made you untouchable. I tried two more times. Around her fourth birthday, and again on her fifth.' She swallowed. 'She was growing so fast. Your assistants refused to put me through.'

Something moved on Graciano's face, an emotion she couldn't comprehend. Did he believe her?

'It's the truth,' she said flatly, something like defiance strengthening her in that moment. 'But don't forget, Graciano, you had turned your back on me a long time ago. Not once did you check on me after that morning. Putting aside the question of pregnancy for a moment,' she said firmly, 'you knew my father was furious. You didn't wonder how that anger might move from you to me? You didn't wonder how he was treating me?'

His mask slipped completely, and she saw that she'd hit a nerve. His eyes swept her face and a muscle jerked at the base of his jaw. 'I presumed with me out of the picture, your life would return to normal.'

'You were wrong.'

'His anger was completely directed at me. I disappeared so his anger would no longer have a target. I was the bad guy who'd taken advantage of his precious daughter…'

'Until I told him the truth,' she said. 'Until I defended you, and then his anger moved to me.'

'I had no idea you'd do that. I don't know *why* you did. What did you stand to gain?'

'How could I not? I didn't want to live in a world where anyone, especially my father, thought those things of you. I *loved* you, Graciano. I couldn't betray you like that. All these years you've thought the worst of me, but you were wrong.'

'Careful, *querida*. We are here discussing a nine-year-old child I knew nothing about. I don't think you can claim the moral high ground just yet.'

'Are you even listening to me?' she asked, infuriated. 'I'm trying to tell you what happened. I'm saying I tried to tell you. *You* were the one who made that impossible.'

'You should have taken out a damned ad in the newspaper,' he muttered. 'I deserved to know about her.'

'Yes,' she agreed. 'And she deserved to know you. But what if you hurt her? What if you rejected her like you did me? Like my father rejected me? All I have ever done is try to protect Annie, to pour all of my love into her so she had what I never did.'

'You cannot have it both ways. Either you tried to tell me, or you didn't. Which is it?'

'How can you think I'd lie about something like that?'

He made a snorting noise. 'Look at where we're standing, what we're discussing.'

'Damn it, Graciano!' Anger burst through Alicia. 'I never wanted this!' She sucked in a deep breath, trying to calm her nerves. 'Let me show you something,' she said through gritted teeth, moving away from Graciano and into a narrow hallway, then up the stairs and into her room. She knew he was right behind her; she felt his presence.

She crouched down and pulled a plastic crate out from under her bed, then unclipped the lid. There were two folders inside. She thrust one at him, too angry to meet his eyes.

He took it, flipping over the cover with the same anger she felt, until he became very still, his eyes devouring the first page, inserted into a plastic slip. It was a newspaper article about him from nine and a half years ago—a small clipping about an award he'd won as a realtor.

His expression shifted, but she couldn't interpret it as he flicked to the next page. Another article, another award, another accolade. Then the articles shifted a little, to speak of his business deals, and the photos changed, too. Now Graciano was rarely snapped without a glamorous woman on his arm. He flicked again, and again, until he reached the end of the folder, the most recent article taken only three months earlier, about the acquisition of a chain of supermarkets in the UK.

'What is it?' he asked, finally, his voice raw.

'It's for Annie.' She wrapped her arms around her torso. 'I tried to tell you about her, but when I couldn't, I started to do this. I wanted the two of you to be connected one day. Or for her to know that I'd tried. I don't know. It just felt…important somehow.' Tears filmed her eyes. 'But in collecting those clippings, I came to understand how much you'd moved on, how your life was in a completely different sphere to mine. I told myself I was glad. I was raising Annie alone, but at least you had what you'd always wanted.'

He stared at the folder, his face ashen.

'And that one?'

Now her fingers really trembled as she crouched down and lifted the second folder. But she held it close to her chest, anxious for some reason to pass it over.

'It's about Annie,' she whispered. 'I wasn't sure if you'd ever want to be a part of her life, but I kept everything, just in case.'

'Show me.' It was a demand. She had saved these things for him, and yet she hesitated a moment, before passing the folder across.

He opened it to the first page—a tiny birth

announcement, a hospital bracelet and a snip of hair sticky taped against an aging slip of cardboard. The next page showed a handprint and footprint.

'She was tiny.'

'She was a month premature,' Alicia said, memories slamming into her.

'Why?'

'I went into labour early.' She didn't meet his eyes; her gaze remained on the folder. Her fingers trembled a little as she lifted the next sheet to turn it. 'This was her first Christmas. Wasn't she adorable? I made that dress.' She ran a finger over the photo, remembering the austerity of that day, the loneliness. Her father hadn't called. He hadn't sent a card, nor a gift. In fact, there'd been no presents whatsoever, but Alicia had had Annie, the love of her life. She was so young in the photo, her face that of a child's.

He turned the page quickly—artwork of Annie's, from when she started nursery. Silly splashes of paint and blobs of colour on cardboard. A student report card. On and on it went, all the small things from her life—piano recital programs, photos of the milestone moments like first lost tooth, riding a bike, and sometimes, Alicia had included a handwritten note about a memory so she wouldn't forget, and wouldn't forget to tell Graciano. All of it had seemed important at the time, but she wondered if he'd understand that.

He came to halfway through the folder, then stopped, lifting his face to hers. 'Can I take this with me?'

She hesitated. 'I made it for you,' she said slowly.

'I won't lose it.'

'I know.' She pressed a finger into the page, strangely sentimental about the memory folder, but it wasn't hers. She'd had Annie, the real thing. This was just a memento. 'Of course.' She stepped back, blinking away the tears, her heart heavy, her soul exhausted.

'I never wanted her to be separated from you.'

'And yet, if I hadn't been at that charity auction, I still wouldn't know about her.'

Alicia grimaced, because that was true.

'I understand why as a sixteen-year-old you couldn't tell me. I take responsibility for my part in that,' he admitted after a beat. 'And even for being almost impossible to contact since. I accept the truth of your explanation.'

'How magnanimous,' she muttered, even as her heart soared with relief.

'But what about on the island, when you had my full attention?'

Her heart dropped to her toes.

'It's very easy to stand here now and say that

you were planning to tell me, when everything has fallen down to circumstance. I happened to be at the charity auction. I happened to be with you when you got the call about Annie's injury. I have to wonder—if those things hadn't happened, would I know about her yet?'

'Yes,' she promised. 'I went to you last night intending to tell you. The truth has been eating me alive. On the island, I couldn't stop thinking about it—'

'Yet you said nothing.'

'It was hardly a straightforward situation,' she said pointedly. 'Sleeping together—'

He moved closer, eyes holding hers, body so close, so large, everything inside her sparked, and she almost cried because she wanted to collapse against him.

'Sleeping together is the only thing that's ever made sense with us,' he muttered.

'At the time, yes, but it always makes things worse afterwards.'

'Does it?' He lifted a hand, catching her cheek. 'Maybe if we never left bed, we'd never fight.'

Her eyes widened, her lips parted, and then he was kissing her, his mouth claiming hers, and it was just as he said: everything made sense. This was exactly what she needed, what made her feel right and complete and as though everything was going to be all right. Her mouth filled with salt as tears rolled down her cheeks—not sad tears so much as tears of acceptance, because he was right. Theirs was a relationship of contradictions, of dependence and need, even when that need terrified them both.

'This doesn't solve anything,' she groaned, even as she pulled him down to the floor.

'No.' His agreement sealed some part of her. She kissed him back with every fibre of her being, even as her heart was turning frozen, made frigid by the impossibility of this.

Their mutual explosion was as powerful as ever, robbing him of sight, sense and the ability to think while it racked his body, and then as he came down on top of her, his weight something she welcomed with a soft groan, he felt as though he'd done something monumentally stupid. Sleeping with Alicia might feel great in the moment, but it just complicated the issue.

They had a daughter. He couldn't seduce his way out of that.

A tidal wave of emotions worked through him, anger at the forefront. But it wasn't just anger at Alicia. It was so much more complicated than that.

He'd fought with her because he hadn't been willing to give any ground, but her words had

worked their way into his soul, and now, he saw
her as the sixteen-year-old she'd been, pregnant
and terrified, then a seventeen-year-old single
mother, and he felt his own failings every step
of the way.

Why hadn't he called to check on her?

Why hadn't he at least made sure her father
hadn't taken his anger out on Alicia once Graciano had left?

Because she was quicksand. Because a conversation could so easily turn into something
more, and he hadn't been willing to let her hurt
him again. He hadn't wanted to let her in.

And now?

'I need to think,' he said, shifting away from
her and standing, frowning as he dressed. Alicia stayed where she was, staring at the ceiling. It was only when he was fully clothed and
he looked at her again that she realised she was
shaking.

He crouched beside her, unable to keep the
concern from his face.

'Shock,' she said in explanation, her face pale.
'I'm fine.'

And he saw her strength then, the strength
she'd needed as Edward Griffiths' daughter, the
strength she'd needed as a teenage mother, and
every day since.

She was quicksand.

He wanted to draw her into his arms, to hold her close, but there were several issues at play here. Being parents to a nine-year-old didn't mean he was willing to open himself up to Alicia and the risks that came with being near her.

'I need to think,' he repeated, and now, she nodded. His eyes shifted to the book she'd made, on the edge of the bed. 'Do you mind if I take that?'

She shook her head. 'I made it for you.' Her eyes stared right through him. 'I wanted—what I wanted wasn't possible, Graciano. But I always intended for you to know.' She bit down on her lip.

He wanted to believe her. Hell, he *did* believe her. But that just made everything worse. He leaned forward, pressing a kiss to her forehead, then standing.

'And eventually, I convinced myself that you'd have wanted it this way. Your life was so…much. It was huge. You were so successful, so far away from us. I told myself you'd want it this way. I meant nothing to you—why should you have to pay for a mistake you made ten years ago?'

That just made it so much worse—that she could even think that of him. A deep, shearing sadness broke him in two. 'I'll be in touch.'

He didn't see the look of concern that crossed her features, but at the door, he turned back to face her and something inside of him shattered. He'd fallen in love with Alicia when she was just a teenager, and she looked so heartbreakingly young now. He stared at her for a moment and then left quickly, before he realised that the thing he wanted most of all was to stay.

CHAPTER TWELVE

GRACIANO CRADLED THE Scotch in the palm of his hand, staring at the collection of memories with an ache low in his gut. He was only four pages in. He couldn't get past Alicia's handwritten note.

Annie is walking. At ten months. All the doctors said she'd be delayed in her milestones because she was born early, but so far that's definitely not the case. She's so sturdy on her feet, so strong and stubborn. She's so like you.

He closed his eyes on a wave of emotion, drinking Scotch simply to clear the knot in his throat. Alicia had written this for him. She'd used the only means possible to share Annie with him. She'd thought of him—with every milestone Annie had achieved. Carefully, he flipped to the back, to a photo of Annie reading a comic book. Closer inspection showed it to be Spanish.

Annie is officially more competent in Spanish than I am. She's beginning to slip between both languages effortlessly. I've worked hard to teach her what I could, but she took it in her stride and has been watching shows in Spanish and reading books, too. She's very bright, but it's more than that. She has Spanish blood, and her tongue knows it. One day, I want to take her there.

He could almost feel her hesitating, feel her emotion.

I want her to see the places I love.

He shut the book at the same time he closed his eyes. These memories were important, but reading about them like this wasn't right. He wanted to hear Alicia's voice recounting the memories to him, describing them in greater depth. He wanted to be able to ask questions, to hear her voice as she answered them. He wanted more.

But what exactly?

His brow beaded in perspiration as he stood, then moved to the window to stare out.

Ten years ago, he'd believed the worst in Alicia. Why hadn't he realised that she'd speak the truth? That of *course* she would defend him? She had been a teenager, sheltered and adored, and until that morning, had idolised her father.

Naturally she hadn't been able to defy him in the moment.

But she'd loved Graciano, too.

He made a growling noise, because she *had* loved him—yet he'd been so quick to judge her. To *hate* her. And up until two nights ago, he'd been willing to make that same mistake.

To prejudge her. To see the worst in her actions.

To fail to listen to her.

To fail her, point-blank.

His shoulders dropped, because the more he looked at their situation, the more he realised he'd messed up.

Alicia stared at the text message for several seconds.

Do you have a minute?

It was so like Graciano, so short and to the point. So unclear, too. Two days earlier, he'd walked out of her home and ever since she'd been tormenting herself with wondering.

What had he meant? What did he need to think about?

In the back of her mind, all she could think of was his reaction in the hospital, his threat that he'd take Annie away to punish her. But then she

emembered the way they'd made love, and the
way he'd been afterwards—surely he couldn't
be so cruel? She gripped her phone more tightly.

Yes. I can talk.

It was almost ten o'clock, but she was nowhere
near ready for bed. She'd barely been sleeping.
She held her phone, waiting for it to ring, but a
moment later, a knock at the front door sounded.
Heart leaping into her throat, Alicia stood, moving quickly to the door, fingers shaking a little
as she slid the chain in place and opened it an
inch. Graciano stood there against the inky black
sky, his dark eyes unsettling her, burning her,
probing her, his face a mask of intense concentration so she was startled.

'I presumed you meant to call me,' she said
quietly.

'No.' Then, with a grimace, 'Would you prefer that?'

She frowned, the question unexpected. 'You're
here now,' she said, casting a glance over her
shoulder. 'Annie's asleep.'

'I presumed she would be—this is a conversation between you and me, not our daughter.'

Our daughter. She shivered, her heart spas-
ming at that simple statement.

Alicia closed the door so she could release

the chain lock, then opened it wider, waving for him to come in. He held Annie's book in his hand, and Alicia felt a tug of sentiment towards that item.

'Through here?' he prompted, nodding towards the living room. It took her a moment to galvanise her limbs into action.

'Right, yes. That way.' They moved through to the lounge and Alicia's eyes fell on her glass of wine. 'Would you like a drink?'

'Thanks.' He dipped his head. She weaved away from him into the kitchen, careful to give Graciano a wide berth or risk igniting with him all over again. But oh, how she craved his touch! The reassurance and familiarity of his arms wrapping around her... 'Wine? Beer? Whisky?'

'Whatever you're having.'

She poured another measure of wine, then passed it over the counter, watching as his long-fingered hand curved around the glass, carrying it back to the sofa. He didn't sit, though.

Alicia reached for her own glass on the coffee table and lifted it to her lips.

'You wanted to talk?'

His eyes bore into hers. 'I think we must, don't you?'

Her throat was dry. This was excruciating. Agony pummelled her. Slowly she nodded, taking another sip of wine before sitting on the edge of the sofa, perched in an almost crouch, ready to spring up if needed. Defensive. Uncertain. Wary.

Graciano placed the folder on the coffee table, staring at it a moment before looking to her. He read her body language like a book, and knowing him to be the cause of those emotions fractured something deep inside of him, causing a fault line he doubted he'd ever be able to repair.

'I have no intention of taking Annie away from you.' The thread he'd made had loomed large in his mind for days.

Her eyes widened and there was some satisfaction in the look of relief that immediately crossed her face.

'It was beneath me to imply it. I'm very, very sorry.'

Her lips parted and her pale, pinched face angled to his. 'It wasn't—' She shook her head in consternation. 'I don't understand. What does that mean?'

'I haven't seen you interact with our daughter for more than a cursory amount,' he said, careful to keep any hint of reproach from the words. 'But I know you. I know who you are, and the kind of mother you would be. I've seen this.' He gestured to the folder. 'You have given her so much.'

Alicia's eyes filled with tears and something

rolled in his gut. He hated seeing her upset. He'd always hated it. So much had clarified for him in the last twenty-four hours and now he wondered how he'd ever been such a stranger to himself, his feelings—how he'd let time and success change him so completely.

'Are you saying—' She looked up at him carefully, then blinked away, her lips pressed together. 'You're leaving?'

He furrowed his brow, not following her logic. 'What?'

'You don't want to be in her life after all?'

He swore in Spanish, then moved towards her, crouching in front of her so their eyes were closer to level. 'That's absolutely *not* what I mean.'

Her gaze roamed his face, trying to understand. 'Then what?'

'I have to explain something to you,' he said after a beat, knowing how important it was to go right back to the beginning. 'You know I told you that leaving you, that first time, was like having the rug pulled from under me? I didn't recognise myself, *querida*. Without you, nothing made sense. Somehow, without me realising it, you became a part of me that summer. I breathed you in, and you weaved through my DNA, so that even when I left Seville, you stayed in me. I hated that. I fought it. Every day, I pushed you away from me. I pushed you out of my mind—my dreams. I willed you away from me with everything I had. I had to. I had to be strong, because if I was weak, I'd go back to you. I'd do whatever it took to be with you, even risk prison.'

'I would *never* have let that happen.'

'Your first instinct was right. You were powerless against your father.'

'He was wrong.'

'Yes,' Graciano agreed. 'But so was I.'

She blinked up at him, then sipped her wine, too fast so she coughed a little. He eased back on his haunches, waiting. 'Why?' she asked, eventually.

'Your father's words were a test of my honour, and I failed it. I ran when I should have stayed and fought. I ran, and in that way, I failed you. I failed the faith you had in me, the love you had given me. I'm sorry.'

She made no effort to disguise her tears now as her lower lip trembled. 'It was a lifetime ago.'

'Was it? Because it feels very much like that failure haunts us both, to this very day.'

She didn't meet his gaze.

'Tell me something, Alicia.'

She blinked at him, her features taut.

'Have you been with anyone since me?'

Alicia's eyes widened and he saw the struggle in them. A moment later, she shook her head slowly. 'But you have. Lots of women.'

'Yes.'

She flinched, and now he could take absolutely no pleasure from her response. Guilt flamed him. 'Physically yes. But I have never become emotionally close with another woman. Not since you.'

Frustration was obvious on her features and then she stood, almost tumbling him backwards, but he gained his balance and stood also. 'So? Nor have I. I haven't been with anyone else since you, Graciano. And before you get ahead of yourself, I don't mean that to stoke your ego. It wasn't about you,' she said. Then, wavering a little, 'Not directly. You broke my heart. You broke it so completely. How could I ever give it to someone else? It wouldn't work. I could never trust another man. I could never let myself believe…in happy endings and roses and romance and promises.' She shook her head angrily. 'Every day with Annie was both a privilege and a torment. I have loved her so much, from the moment I learned I was pregnant, but she has been a constant reminder of you, too.'

'I haven't forgotten about you either, Alicia,' he said urgently. 'You are the only woman I've ever loved, the only woman I've ever truly given myself to. If I broke your heart, you stole mine, and when I left you, I failed to bring it with me.'

She spun away from him, his words not

changing her countenance one iota. She was still angry.

'Stop. Just stop. I'm not an idiot, Graciano.'

'I know that.'

She turned back to him. 'Then don't treat me like one.'

'How am I doing that?'

'I know you've taken your time to get your ducks in a row. Did your lawyers advise you you'd never get sole custody? Is that it? So now you're trying to ingratiate yourself with me to be a part of Annie's life?'

He shouldn't have been surprised that she believed something so low of him, but still, it cut deep. It showed him just how far he had to go in earning back her trust.

'You don't need to do that,' she said, grinding her teeth. 'I never intended to keep you from her. If you want to see her, that's fine, so long as we come up with a way that works for Annie. That's all I care about.'

'Actually, my lawyers advised me—' he saw her face tighten and quickly edited what he'd been about to say '—that it would not necessarily go as you imagine.'

Her eyes swept shut and he felt the fear radiating off her. He swore internally, moving towards her until she flinched.

He hated himself in that moment.

He had done this to her.

He was pulling at the threads of her life, after she'd fought so hard to piece it together. He couldn't do this to her.

He sought for the best way to explain what he'd come to say and in the end settled on the simplest. 'I love you.'

Her face squeezed up.

'Ten years ago, you became a part of me, and you still are. I want Annie in my life and I want you in my life. That's what I came here to say.'

He waited, his nerves pulling taut as he stared at her, until she shook her head sadly.

'No, you don't.'

He frowned.

'The other night, at your place in Knightsbridge, you told me you wanted to hang out for as long as it took to get this out of our system. Before you knew about Annie, you were prepared to allow me only a very limited space in your life.'

He swore aloud this time. 'What I said does not accord with how I felt. I was just too much of a fool to understand that then.'

For a moment, he thought he might have got through to her, but after a beat, she pulled a sad face. 'Do you have any idea what it's like to be a single parent?'

He shook his head slowly.

'It's hard,' she said on a sob. 'Every day. And it's

rewarding and wonderful and I know I shouldn't complain, because you've missed so much, but you have to understand: I have fought to be here, to give her this.' She waved a hand around. 'I love our daughter, and I would always, always choose the life I have over what you're offering.'

The rejection dug into him, making it difficult to breathe for a moment. But he wasn't getting through to her. She didn't believe him.

'Tell me this,' he said quietly, sipping his wine, then replacing it on the coffee table. 'Do you love me?'

She jerked her head back as though he'd struck her and he waited, knowing Alicia wouldn't lie. It was a trap—unfair, but necessary.

'I—' She rolled her lips together. 'I'm a realist,' she said after a beat. 'I understand the limitations of our circumstances.'

'Do you? Because when I look inside at my own heart and feelings, I see only possibilities. For ten years I have run away from you, and I have hated every day. Even my biggest successes have been overshadowed by personal misery. There is one perfect person on this planet, designed to be my other half, and I have been fighting that knowledge to the point I have been barely myself. So to imagine a future not only with you but with our daughter—this is not a limitation, but a world we could inhabit, if we were brave enough to step into it together.'

'Don't talk to me about brave,' she said on a shiver. 'I've been brave. I was brave when I found out about our baby, when I tried to tell you, again and again, when you said those awful things, when you started dating anyone with a vagina in Spain, when you went from strength to strength and all my professional ambitions withered and died. Do you have any idea what it was like when I had my baby, alone in hospital, no one with me except a midwife? And then Di came into my life as my saviour. I have been brave for a long time,' she said stoically, lifting her chin, then fixing him with a defiant expression and wobbling lips.

'I hate that you went through that,' he groaned, the truth wrenched from him. 'What can I say or do, Alicia? I stuffed up. Again and again. Every day that I fought my need for you I have hurt you. I see that. I acknowledge it, and I want to fix it. I have ruined the last ten years, but surely our future is still worth fighting for?'

Her chest shuddered as she inhaled. 'I can't do it,' she said with a small shake of her head. 'I'm so scared, Graciano. After you left, I changed. Trusting people doesn't come easily and you—'

'I know.' He couldn't bear to hear another description of his shortcomings. 'I'm not asking you to trust me all at once,' he said slowly, moving towards her.

'Then what are you asking me for?'

'A date,' he said, his eyes holding a challenge. He lifted a finger between them. 'One date. If you enjoy it, if you enjoy spending time with me, I will ask you for another. And another. And another. And as many dates as it takes for you to understand that my love for you is as real now as it was ten years ago. For as long as it takes for you to understand that I'm sorry. I will never disappoint you again, *querida*.'

'And Annie?'

'For now, she'll know me only as your friend,' he said, knowing he couldn't afford to alienate Alicia on this score. 'I would like to meet her,' he said, cautiously, eyeing her, wondering if that was too much. 'If you're comfortable with that.'

She nodded unevenly, her eyes moving to the folder. He could feel her uncertainty, and he took a step towards the door. 'You let me know when you're free,' he said quietly. 'And I'll arrange something. Okay?'

She bit down on her lower lip. 'I—okay.' Then, taking a step towards the coffee table, she gestured to the book. 'Would you like to look at her folder together?'

Something inside his chest leaped. Hope. Desperate, aching hope. 'Are you sure?'

She nodded. 'I want to share it with you.'

By the time they reached the pages surrounding Annie's sixth birthday, it was almost midnight, and Graciano's words had been going around and around in Alicia's head for a long time.

She closed the folder, lifting her face to his. They were so close it was almost impossible to fight the urge to kiss him.

'The thing is,' she said, eyes on his lips. 'I do love you, you know.'

It was relief that marked his features, not the triumph she'd expected.

'That is very good news.'

'But I can't...risk feeling like I did back then.'

'And you don't trust me?'

She tilted her lips to the side, considering that. 'Honestly? I don't know. But... I haven't dated anyone, ever, really. It sounds kind of fun.'

'You, my darling, deserve to be dated until your feet spin off the earth. It would be my pleasure.' He moved closer then, brushing his lips over hers in a chaste kiss. 'Thank you.'

'What for?'

'A second chance I'm pretty sure I don't deserve.'

'Everyone deserves a second chance.'

EPILOGUE

'You know, I thought you meant the movies, or dinner. Maybe a walk afterwards.'

'We can definitely walk if you'd prefer,' he grinned, leaning back a little so it was the most natural thing in the world for Alicia to lean back into Graciano's chest, to rest her head on his shoulder and sigh as she looked overhead. It was only their third date, but she already knew that her heart belonged to him, just as his did to her.

'Maybe,' she said, happy right where she was. 'We'll see.'

Stars shimmered overhead, more visible here in the Spanish countryside than London. She looked up at them, remembering a long-ago version of herself and the stars that had blanketed the sky the night they made love.

He'd recreated so much of that evening, from the strawberries to the birthday cupcakes to the weather—though she suspected that wasn't in Graciano's control. He'd added a bottle of delightful champagne to the mix, and some Belgian chocolates.

Plus, the property they were on was his—all his. They'd spent the afternoon touring it, from the grand old house to the farm surrounds, seeing the chickens and llamas, the goats, meeting his manager.

'I had no idea you were into all this,' she said, shaking her head.

'As a child, I loved animals,' he said. 'I wanted to be a vet.'

'You're kidding?'

'No.' His eyes roamed her face. 'We had a dog, Brisa. She never stopped—hence the name.'

'Breeze?'

'Yes.' He kissed the tip of her nose. 'We could not contain her, no matter how hard we tried. One day, she got out. A car hit her.'

Alicia turned to face him, sadness softening her features.

'I found her first. I was powerless to save her. I wanted to. Only six months later, there came the accident. I watched my parents die. All I could think of was that I wanted to grow up to be strong, to be knowledgeable.' He shook his head. 'A child's whim.'

'I don't know,' she said, shaking her head. 'The money you donated to McGiven House has saved a lot of people from fates worse than death.'

He squeezed her hand. 'It is a worthy charity.'

She lifted her shoulders. 'They help people who need it most.'

'People like you were, at one time?'

She nodded slowly. 'I don't know what I would have done without my grandmother's generosity.'

It was a sore point and she felt Graciano flinch. She understood. She lifted up, kissing him gently. He wrapped his arms around her, holding her tight.

'I know what I would like to do, for our next date.'

'Oh? What's that?'

'It's a surprise.'

Three days later, during Annie's school hours, Graciano flew Alicia back to Spain—this time, to his charity headquarters.

'I had no idea you did all this,' she said, shocked.

'By design. I don't need people to see this side of me.'

'The secret philanthropist?'

'Money is a burden,' he said after a pause. 'I have more than I could ever spend. More than I could spend in a thousand lifetimes, in fact. There are some people who cannot afford to feed their children.'

Alicia sighed. 'Your heart is big.'

'My heart is yours.'

'I know.'

* * *

For their fifth date, Graciano arrived at Alicia's early, while she was still getting ready. He'd planned it that way, and for a man like Graciano, things almost always went according to plan.

Diane was in the kitchen, finishing dinner for herself and Annie, who was still upstairs doing her homework.

'I wanted to speak to you,' Graciano said, walking into the kitchen but keeping a respectful distance. Here, this was Diane's domain, and where the older woman had been polite to him, Graciano knew he had a long way to go with her yet. She'd seen Alicia broken; she'd picked up the pieces. If anything, Graciano loved that she was still protecting Alicia, even when Graciano would make sure no one ever hurt a hair on her or Annie's head, ever again.

'Yes, Graciano?' Diane's voice was cool but polite. He had to hide his smile.

'You know how I feel about her.'

Diane lifted a brow. 'Do I?'

'Si.'

Diane lifted a single brow. 'The important thing is, does she?'

'I think so. And tonight, I'm going to be sure of it.' He reached into his pocket and pulled out the ring box, sliding it across the counter. Nerves assailed him.

Diane eyed the box, hesitated a moment and then lifted it. She cracked the lid, making a low, whistling sound.

'Goodness, I think I'm blind.'

Graciano dragged a hand over his stubble. 'Too much?'

Diane laughed—the first time he'd heard the noise from the older woman. 'I mean, it'll be visible from the moon…'

Graciano stared at it. Maybe he'd gone too far?

'Perhaps I should change it.'

Diane reached over, putting a hand on his. 'Pish, it's perfect. I'm only messing with you—I think you deserve a little of that, don't you? She'll love it.'

'I just wanted her to know…to really understand…'

'She will,' Di assured him.

Graciano cleared his throat, taking the ring back from Diane's outstretched hand. 'So, do I have your approval?'

'Are you asking me if you can propose?'

Graciano shrugged, feeling completely stupid now. None of these were familiar emotions, but then, everything about life since he'd confided his feelings in Alicia had been new and scary, but also absolutely wonderful.

Diane laughed properly then at Alicia's faraway voice calling down, asking what was going on. Graciano threw Di a warning look and she covered her mouth.

'Sorry,' she replied, *sotto voce*. 'It is certainly not my place to give you permission. She's her own woman and always has been.' A sheen of tears moistened Diane's eyes, and there was rich affection in her features. 'But if you're asking if I approve, the answer is yes.'

Graciano expelled a slow breath.

'I've seen how happy you make her. I've always cared for her, you know, but it's only in the last few weeks I've realised that I knew a very small part of her. She's been waiting for you. Don't make her wait any longer.'

The helicopter came in over his island and Alicia, blindfolded beside him, jiggled her fingers in her lap. He couldn't stop smiling.

They loved each other. It was mutual and absolute. And tonight, he intended to formalise that.

Only he hoped and prayed she'd say yes, that it wasn't too soon—that she wasn't still weighing up her future.

But if she was, that was okay. He'd wait. He'd be here, enjoying her, loving her, for as long as she let him.

'Where are we?' she said on a smile, her lips

so full and curved that he couldn't help himself. He leaned forward and kissed her gently, so she smiled against him.

'Wherever it is, I'm happy.'

'Good.'

The helicopter thudded down and a moment later the door was opened.

'Ready?'

'You betcha.'

He removed the blindfold as the golf buggy pulled up beside the helicopter. It took her a moment to realise what was happening.

'Your island?'

'Someone organised a very elaborate party. I didn't want it to go to waste.'

She frowned, confused. 'You want me to come to the party as your date?'

'You are the party,' he said.

She stared at him, shocked. 'That's… You can't be serious.'

But he was. Every element she'd organised had been scaled back to suit two guests. There was food, dancing, champagne, and when the barge just out from the island began to release the fireworks, Graciano went down on one knee, squeezing her hand to draw her attention to him.

'There is no one on this earth I love like I do you. In every way, for all time, since we first met, you have been my other half. I was foolish and arrogant and I will never be able to change our past, but you are my future, Alicia. You and Annie are the meaning to my world. I know it's soon, but having wasted ten years, I can't wait another night. Will you marry me?'

She stared first at his face and then at the ring he'd opened a box to reveal, and tears sparkled on her lashes—tears of such happiness. 'I never thought this would be our ending,' she said. 'All those nights spent missing you, wondering where you were, worrying for you, loving you without purpose and hope...'

'There is always hope,' he corrected, standing so he could draw her into an embrace. 'With a heart so full as yours, there is always hope.'

He slid the ring onto her finger and she stared down at it, mesmerised by the enormous, sparkling gem, but also by the future they were stepping towards. Everything about this moment, his proposal, felt absolutely perfect.

One year later, Mrs Alicia Cortéz had the pleasure of telling her husband of six months that they were to be parents again—and this time, together. Their journey would be a shared one, every step of the way. Their time was split between Spain and London. Both would have preferred to relocate to Spain full-time, but Annie had a life in London, and there was Diane to consider, now as dear a friend to Graciano as she always had been to Alicia. When their baby boy was born, it was Diane who oversaw his medical needs, and a month later, Diane who was named their son's godmother.

Graciano could only look at his family with gratitude for the second chance he'd been given. A third baby would someday bless them, but before she was born, Graciano received a call that would change his life for ever.

He answered his phone on the third ring, watching his wife and daughter play with his little boy, his heart stretched to a wonderful breaking point.

'Cortéz?'

'Speaking.'

'It's Caleb James.'

Graciano, momentarily, drew a blank. 'Yes?'

'The investigator, from Washington.'

It had been so long since he'd engaged the man—of course he'd forgotten. He'd seen a bill from time to time, and had been content to let the matter tick along in the background on the basis that maybe, one day, he'd get lucky and something about his brother would turn up.

'Can I help you?'

'I think I've got something.'

Graciano stood straighter. 'You think, or you know?'

Out of the corner of his eye, he saw Alicia shift, her face turning to his, curiosity on her features. They were so in tune it was predictable that she'd hear his voice and worry.

'I'm ninety-nine percent sure.'

'What is it?'

'I believe your brother is in Savisia.'

'The Middle East? Why?'

'I'm still looking into that, but the theory holds together.'

'I don't want "holds together",' Graciano said, shaking his head. 'I want watertight.'

'Let me tell you what I've got.' He proceeded to outline the working theory. When the accident occurred, the sheikh of Savisia was touring Spain with his young wife. We don't know much, but they donated a large sum to the hospital to keep everything off the books and your brother seems to have gone home with them. This all checks out—the dates, their visit, the two-million-pound donation.'

Graciano closed his eyes. 'My brother disappeared off the radar. It explains why no adoption agency has ever heard of him. Why I couldn't find him.'

'What about the American connection?'

'Best I can guess, they used an American senator's private jet to fly him out—a diplomatic favour.'

Graciano swore.

'I have a photo of him.'

'Send it to me.'

The investigator paused. 'I will. But before you open it, there are two things you should know.'

'Yes?'

'Your brother was very young.'

'I'm aware of that.'

'He suffered a lot of trauma in the accident. Preliminary reports suggest his memory may have been affected by his injuries. That would explain why they were able to take him.'

'And why my visit was upsetting to him,' Graciano said, piecing it together.

'Yes.'

'You said there were two things I should know?'

'Your brother is now the ruling sheikh of Savisia. He may not welcome a voice from his past, challenging his right to the throne.'

Graciano gripped the phone tight, staring at his family with all the love in his heart. 'He will,' he said, nodding confidently.

'How can you be so sure?'

'Because I've recently become a believer in second chances.'

* * * * *